"Adriana, I am so sorry to hear about your father. I was going to call, but I didn't want to intrude. I was also worried that it was the situation with Stella that may have triggered his attack, and I wasn't sure if my call would be welcome. How is he?"

"He is stable. They are going to put a stent in, and they think with proper care he should recover and hopefully not have another attack. As for what caused it, there is no point in speculating. Anyway, that's not why I'm here."

"Of course not." Rob studied her face. "So why are you here? If I can help in any way, of course I will." He hesitated. "But I won't marry Stella. If that's what you are here to suggest. While I am sorry for what has happened, that wouldn't be right."

"I know. That's not why I am here. I..." All her carefully rehearsed speeches vanished clear out of her head. "I want you to marry me instead. I'm proposing a merger."

Dear Reader,

My family are very important to me for entirely personal reasons.

In this book, the idea of family is central, but for Rob and Adriana, it is more than personal—it is all about duty and responsibility. Love hasn't come into it, and they are determined it won't.

They both believe that their happy-ever-after is one that can be negotiated into being, built on a foundation of convenience.

But as they plan and parley on the beautiful island of Madeira, somehow love does its best to come to the bargaining table.

In the end, Rob and Adriana have to make a choice between duty and love. I hope you enjoy discovering which they choose.

Nina x

Falling for His Stand-In Fiancée

Nina Milne

Recycling programs
for this product may
not exist in your area.

ISBN-13: 978-1-335-73683-3

Falling for His Stand-In Fiancée

Copyright © 2022 by Nina Milne

Harlequin Enterprises ULC
22 Adelaide St. West, 41st Floor
Toronto, Ontario M5H 4E3, Canada
www.Harlequin.com

Printed in U.S.A.

Nina Milne has always dreamed of writing for Harlequin Romance—ever since she played libraries with her mother's stacks of Harlequin romances as a child. On her way to this dream, Nina acquired an English degree, a hero of her own, three gorgeous children and—somehow!—an accountancy qualification. She lives in Brighton and has filled her house with stacks of books—her very own *real* library.

Books by Nina Milne

Harlequin Romance

The Casseveti Inheritance

Italian Escape with the CEO
Whisked Away by the Italian Tycoon
The Secret Casseveti Baby

A Crown by Christmas

Their Christmas Royal Wedding

Conveniently Wed to the Prince
Hired Girlfriend, Pregnant Fiancée?
Whisked Away by Her Millionaire Boss
Baby on the Tycoon's Doorstep
Second Chance in Sri Lanka

Visit the Author Profile page
at Harlequin.com for more titles.

To my family with love xx

Praise for
Nina Milne

"*Their Christmas Royal Wedding* is an escapist, enjoyable and emotional contemporary tale that will touch readers' hearts with its beguiling blend of searing intensity, heart-warming drama and uplifting romance. Nina Milne writes with plenty of warmth and heart and she has penned a poignant and spellbinding romantic read."

—*Goodreads*

CHAPTER ONE

THE HONOURABLE ADRIANA MORRISON looked up as she heard the sound of her name being called. Damn! She'd been sure that she'd be alone for the next few hours. Swiftly she covered the easel and moved it out of sight into a small alcove, pulled the curtain across. Glanced down at herself—thankfully she'd only just got started, so there was no paint on her as yet.

She glanced round the room for any tell-tale signs of her artistic endeavours and, once satisfied there weren't, she walked to the door and pulled it open, smiled at her elder sister with the familiar mix of love tinged with the tiniest hint of envy that, try as she might, Adriana couldn't shift. However much she loved Stella.

And she did try, understood that it wasn't Stella's fault that she was beautiful, smart, vivacious and all-round perfect. Nor was it her sister's fault that she was the loved one, the child who could do no wrong, the daughter her father adored, in so much as Lord Salvington was capable of adoring anyone.

Whereas their father literally couldn't bear the sight of Adriana, the daughter who should have been the son he longed for. The son he had been promised—the gender scan had been sure she would be a boy. Sometimes Adriana tried to picture the moment Lord Salvington had been told he had a second daughter, the bitter disappointment, the anger and rage etched on those sneering features. Compounded by the fact her mother had suffered such complications during the birth that she would never fall pregnant again.

The all too familiar stab of guilt pinched at her and she shook her head to dislodge the thoughts. Her brain knew it was not her fault she was a girl, that she deserved her father's love regardless of her sex, that she hadn't intended to put a stop to future pregnancies. But years of witnessing her father's disappointment, years of watching her parents' marriage disintegrate, years of her father's constant putdowns and her mother's sadness told her that it *was* her fault. Because, unwittingly or not, she was the cause, the catalyst that had led her family down a path strewn with misery and bitterness.

And, unwittingly or not, she was the reason that Salvington could pass to some distant cousin who knew how many times removed. A man called Bobby Galloway, an American who had no interest at all in being 'lumbered' with the responsibilities of an estate and had been clear he would sell Salvington to the highest bidder.

Adriana understood her father's deep sadness, frustration and anger that this should happen, all due to an archaic, outdated system that insisted on male primogeniture, decreed that the estate and title pass down the male line. To give him his due he had fought tirelessly to try to change that system, so that Stella could somehow inherit. That had been Strategy A. His Strategy B had been a disaster, a cold-hearted affair, a 'try before you buy' attempt to get another woman pregnant that culminated in a scandal that rocked their house. Because when a scan revealed the sex to be a girl, Lord Salvington had rejected the woman, who went public with the story. Adriana could still feel the sear of sorrow and shame and misery. Made worse when the woman had lost the baby. After that for some reason her father's dislike of his second daughter had intensified. As if the failure of Strategy B was her fault.

Thank goodness for her mother and her sister, who both loved her and did their best to protect her. Though Stella was always careful not to show love or kindness to her sister in front of their father. The sisters had learnt early on that that was the way to infuriate Lord Salvington and trigger the caustic edge of his tongue against both Adriana and their mother. That the best course of action was for Adriana to be as invisible as possible.

But that didn't stop them from forging a real bond, and now worry touched Adriana as she took in the pallor of her sister's face, the panic that clouded the beautiful blue eyes. 'What's wrong?' She glanced at her watch. 'And what are you doing here?' Stella was supposed to be on her way for her first date with Rob Wilmington, Viscount Rochester, heir to the Earldom of Darrow.

A different type of envy, a different type of guilt threatened to surface and Adriana pushed it down. The fact that she had once harboured some sort of foolish crush on the man destined to marry her sister was a secret she planned to take to the grave. Even more so as the whole thing had been toe-curlingly stupid, the only saving grace being she was sure Rob had never suspected. In truth it was extremely unlikely that Rob even remembered her.

'I can't go through with it.' Stella's voice was low, the words so utterly unexpected that Adriana was sure she must have misheard.

'Sorry?'

'You heard me.' Stella came in, started to pace in front of the battered mahogany desk.

'What do you mean? It's all arranged; you're the one who planned the whole thing.'

'I know,' Stella wailed. 'And I meant to do it, Ria, I really did. I *wanted* to do it.'

Adriana tried to think; she truly had not seen this coming. The proposed marriage had been welcomed by Stella as the 'grand alliance' she'd always been destined for. Always wanted. A duty she welcomed. For this was Strategy C. Although the Salvington estate and title could not pass directly to a daughter, due to a legal quirk set back in the history of time, it could pass on to the male offspring of a daughter, provided that offspring was born 'in wedlock' and was born whilst the existing Lord was alive. So it had always been essential, if Strategies A and B failed, that Stella would marry and have a son and heir. In addition their father expected a 'good' marriage, wanted his heir to be worthy, with the correct blood running through his veins.

Stella had been happy to go along with that, bound by a duty to her ancestral home. In the past weeks she'd surrounded herself with bridal magazines and pictured her life as the future Countess of Darrow. Her only stipulation that, although the marriage was to be one of convenience, it would appear to be a love match. She and Rob would be the fairy-tale aristocratic couple, present the celebrity magazines with interviews and photographs, attend balls and dinners. Stella had surely been looking forward to bridal glory and today should have been the first sweeping step towards that. A romantic lunch in one of Oxford's most expensive restaurants. Champagne and a discreetly alerted journalist in attendance.

'I don't understand. What's happened? What's changed?'

Stella twisted her hands together. 'I'm pregnant.'

'What?' Shock conflated with confusion. 'But if you and Rob are…'

'It's not Rob's. He and I haven't even kissed.' Stella gave a strangled laugh. 'I had that planned for date number three in full view of the press. We were going to hold hands at date two. A peck on the cheek was scheduled for today—date one.'

'But…' Adriana's brain desperately tried to compute the information. 'Then who *is* the father?'

'It doesn't matter.'

'Yes, it does. It matters a lot, given our situation. Are you going to marry him?' That way, at least, if the baby was a boy there would be an heir.

Stella's strides increased. 'No. That is not an option. But neither is marrying Rob. I can't pretend the baby is his.'

Adriana studied her sister. 'But you thought about it?' she asked, keeping all judgement from her voice. 'Is that why you've left it this late to pull out of this date?'

'I only did the test today. I know that was stupid, but I thought… I *hoped* I would be wrong. I even thought if I were to be pregnant it wouldn't matter. I'd have an abortion. But now…' She rested her hand on her tummy. 'Now…now I know it's a disaster but I want to keep the baby.' She stopped. 'Please don't give me a hard time. I know I've messed up, messed up our whole plan, but I'll make it right somehow in the future…'

'Whoa. Slow down. I'm not going to give

you a hard time—I would never do that. You're my sister and you've always been the best sister I could wish for.' The plan had been concocted when they were young, when they'd vowed to save their ancestral home somehow and to share it.

It was decided that one day Stella would be Lady of the Manor, carry out all the high-society duties, be the public face of Salvington, whilst Adriana would do what she loved most: look after the land and manage the estate.

'As for the plan, you don't need to worry about that right now. Because we have far bigger worries. If you don't go through with marrying Rob, Father is going to go ballistic.'

Her own fear was reflected on Stella's face, a fear that she had lived with all her life, an underlay of darkness that clouded the brightest day. Fear of her father's anger.

Though once, apparently, her father had been a different man. Kind and loving; their parents' marriage had been a love match and often Lady Salvington would look back, tell Adriana of their happiness, their courtship, had described a man Adriana could not imagine as her father.

Because disappointment over the lack of an heir had curdled love with bitterness; and slowly, slowly, as the barren years had passed love had morphed into dislike and a need to belittle; vitriolic words that put his wife and daughter 'in their place'. Stella and Adriana had often begged their mother to leave but she had refused, too scared that she would lose custody. Known too how much both sisters loved their ancestral home—felt too that it would be wrong to take them from it even if she did.

So, life continued and Adriana kept herself as invisible as possible. Spent hours away from the family, roaming the estate or shut away painting. Painting landscapes of Salvington, trying to capture the beauty and reality of a place she loved, a place she felt she had in some way let down. Her art, the silver lining to her cloud, a means of expressing her feelings, a hobby she loved and told no one about. Refused to expose something precious to her to the sneers and derision of her father.

But now there would be worse than derision—and when Lord Salvington discovered his favourite child had failed him, that Plan C was down the pan, there was no strategy that would stem the tide of his anger.

'What are we going to do?'

'I'll have to tell Father,' Stella said. 'And

there's another problem,' Stella said. 'Rob will be in the restaurant by now.'

'You need to tell him. We can't leave him stranded.'

'I know.' Stella frowned, resumed pacing. 'The problem is, I've got press all lined up to catch us. I've dropped all the right hints and I'm pretty sure there will be at least one celebrity journalist in that restaurant to scoop us. So they will see him take my call, or get my text.' Her stride increased. 'I can't think straight. But if the press get even a glimmer of suspicion about my condition, then...'

'We are up the creek without a paddle or a stick.'

'More than you know. I can't risk the paternity of this baby coming out. I can't.' Stella's voice broke. 'But there is one thing we could do...'

Rob Wilmington, Viscount Rochester, heir to the Earldom of Darrow, glanced surreptitiously at his watch. Where was Stella? He could only assume she was planning a grand entrance. Not for the first time he questioned the idea of a public 'romance'.

He understood that a positive, happy spin would hopefully undo the horrible negativity of scandal for both families. Even now, two years later, he could taste the bitter tang of his own humiliation. Recalled seeing Emily, his fiancée, the woman he'd loved, splashed across the tabloids locked in a passionate embrace with her ex-boyfriend.

So he'd agreed to Stella's suggestion, understood, too, her point when she'd said, *'I have no wish for true romance but I would like to enjoy the trappings of it.'* So she'd planned a campaign, laid a trail so that their first date would garner some publicity, had the whole next few weeks mapped out.

As for Rob, he had no interest in romance whatsoever. Would never be fool enough to make the mistake of believing in love again.

He'd risked everything for Emily; at one point his parents had even threatened to disinherit him, they had been so dismayed by his declaration of love for a girl so far 'below them'. But Rob truly hadn't cared, hadn't thought her background mattered a jot. So what if she came from a rough council estate, so what if her father and brother had done time in prison, so what if her past boyfriends left a lot to be desired?

And he still didn't believe any of that mattered. What had mattered was the fact that, whilst he loved Emily, that love hadn't been reciprocated; Emily had been taking him for a ride, had joined the train because she expected glamour and riches, had been dazzled by his title and position. Shades of his parents in a way. They loved him because he was an heir, and would ensure the Darrow line remained unbroken for at least another generation. Before his birth they had all but given up hope of having an heir, after years of miscarriages and failed treatments, and then he'd come along, late in their lives, a 'miracle baby'. They had never seen him as an individual in his own right, he was a treasured commodity to be moulded to continue in the traditions of all the Earls of Darrow. As a result, in the name of love and duty they had tried to control his life. Decided it was too risky for him to ride a bike, had sent him to boarding school, but with the diktat that he wasn't allowed to play rugby, go swimming, do anything in case he got injured.

But at least they loved him in their own way. Emily hadn't. When his back was turned, she'd hooked up with her ex, fresh out of prison and more than happy to make a quick legitimate buck from the press. Once it was out in the open and Rob had wised up, the ex convinced

Emily to jump on his bandwagon and they milked the scandal for all it was worth.

When he recalled some of the 'truth' Emily had revealed, the intimate details, hot anger still welled up, not only with her but also with himself for falling for her act. The pretence of passion, the fakery of love. When in fact, as she had so cheerfully admitted to all and sundry, she'd been 'lying back and thinking of her ex', although she'd felt so bad. 'I tried, I really did,' she explained, 'because Rob is a decent man, a man who was trying so hard.' Pause and a small, cheeky smile. 'I didn't mean it like that.'

Enough. Not now. It was over. He'd been a fool once…he wouldn't be again. After Emily he had decided to take control of his life, wouldn't let anyone call the shots any more. He would do his duty because it was the right thing to do but on his own terms. First he'd brokered a deal with his parents. That he would go away for two years, but then he would come back, settle down, create an heir, take over the running of the estate, so his parents could semi-retire, spend more time in their villa in Portugal, stand down after a lifetime of dedication to Darrow.

But he knew he wanted more than to continue in their footsteps, knew he wanted to forge his own path. The knowledge was reinforced in his two years away. Because he had revelled in the freedom of being plain Rob Wilmington. He'd enrolled on a business course, a creative design course, a web design course and somewhere along the way an idea had germinated for a business. An idea he'd run with, with the help of a fellow student, Fleur Hardcastle, and for which he'd got funding, and he knew Easel Enterprises would be a winner—he knew it in his gut.

And he took pride from the fact it had been set up by plain Rob Wilmington, only Fleur had known that he was an English aristocrat. And soon the company would launch properly, taken forward by Fleur. He'd decided to remain in the background, as a consultant for now. Because it was time to keep his promise to his parents, time to take on the mantle of duty. Because he understood his parents' need for continuity. They were in their early seventies, they wanted to see a next heir, to know the Earldom would continue.

But once he'd got married, once he'd got the hang of the estate, Rob intended to also have a life of his own. Intended to take Easel Enterprises to great things.

But that was in the future; first the marriage. A marriage of convenience, as he would never give any woman power over him again, the power to inflict hurt or humiliation. This would be a partnership, a mutually beneficial arrangement, part of his aristocratic life.

So here he was. The question was, where was Stella? Unease touched him as he resisted the urge to pull out his phone and check for messages. Where was she? Here he was, ready to play Romeo—all he needed was the other half of the duo.

He looked up as the glass revolving door of the on-trend Oxford restaurant swung open, allowing in a blast of air and the noise of the shoppers that thronged outside. His gaze landed on the woman who came in. Not Stella—the hair not blonde, the clothes not right.

Instead this woman had shoulder-length light-brown hair, with an overlong fringe, her shoulders were ever so slightly hunched and she looked more than a little apprehensive. Realising that his gaze had lingered on her way too long, he looked away and then back again as a definite sense of familiarity struck him. He knew who she was—of course he did.

And it wasn't only him who had worked out

her identity; he sensed the interest of a couple sitting at an adjoining table, wondered if they were from a paper.

Before he could work out what to do, she brushed her fringe from her eyes, straightened up and hurried towards the table.

'Rob.'

On automatic, he rose to his feet, the welcoming smile stuck in place. What the hell was going on? Just as she stumbled. Instinctively he moved to catch her, and as his arms went round her waist he felt a sudden unmistakeable jolt of awareness, so unexpected he froze. Recovered himself, gently steadied her and stepped back, saw heat tinge her skin, and as his gaze met hers he saw an answering response before she looked down.

'Adriana? Is Ste—?'

Before he could finish the sentence she rushed into speech. 'Hello, Rob, I am so sorry I am late—and on our first date as well. But I am so glad to be here now.'

Rob blinked. Right. The options were that he was going nuts and had mixed up the sisters. This seemed unlikely. But there had to be some reason for Adriana to be here. Another brush of her fringe showed large grey eyes that now surveyed him with a hint of apprehension and an unmistakeable plea. All too aware of the glances from the neighbouring table, he decided he'd play along. Though an underlay of anger rippled inside him; he didn't like being manipulated and this stank to high heaven of exactly that. Even worse, it was in full view of the press.

'Don't worry at all—I'm glad you made it.' He kept his voice smooth, saw her small exhalation of relief.

As she sat down he took the opportunity to study her properly; he hadn't seen her recently—for one reason or another she hadn't attended the family dinner that had been part of the pre-romance campaign. But he did remember their encounter from a few years back. It had been a party at Salvington Manor, perhaps a birthday party for Stella. He'd spotted her then, intrigued by how different the sisters were. Unlike Stella, Adriana shunned the limelight, seemed to flit about in the shadows, tidying up, almost as though she wished to render herself invisible.

He'd found her in the kitchen. 'I'm sorry, Stella isn't in here,' she'd said.

'Don't be sorry,' he'd said. 'I'm more than happy to find you.'

That had elicited a smile, one that spoke of

disbelief but also appreciation. 'That's kind of you,' she said.

'I didn't say it to be kind. Why don't I help you with this?'

And for the next fifteen minutes he had done exactly that, chatted as he helped tidy away glasses, loaded the dishwasher, watched as she restocked the fridge, put snacks and canapes on trays.

'So how come you are doing all this?' he asked. There were hired caterers and he was sure there would be additional staff available.

She shrugged. 'I'm not really a party person. I prefer to have something to do and then it's not so obvious I'm not socialising. And anyway…'

She broke off as her sister entered the kitchen, a wide smile on her face, blonde hair rippling past her shoulders. 'There you are, Rob. We've been looking for you. We're about to start a game of Jenga.' Stella turned to her sister. 'Rob is apparently king of the wooden blocks. Come on, Ria—join us.'

'Thank you but I'm actually a bit tired, and you know how bad I am—I don't want to ruin it for everyone.' Rob frowned, watched as Adriana seemed to almost step back into the shadows. Her voice perfectly friendly but it held no hint of regret, her smile for her sister both sweet and absolute.

He hesitated, about to ask again if she was sure, but before he could she'd turned and headed for the door. 'Thanks for the help, Rob. Enjoy the game. I hope you win.'

But he hadn't. Had in fact spent the next hour vaguely unsettled, distracted by those large eyes, the sudden sweet smile, the wariness and reserve in her expression.

But that was then and this was now. Odd, though, how clear that memory was. As he studied her he realised in some ways little had changed. There was still the overlong fringe that drew attention away from her face, yet now he could see how striking her features were, wondered why she wore her hair in a way that obscured them. Her grey eyes were large and the colour of a stormy sea. It was a face that would age well, keep its classic cast. Her nose aquiline straight, her lips generous and…as his gaze lingered on them he suddenly became aware of what he was doing. Enough. Why on earth was he checking her out? Noticing her mouth, the gloss of her hair? When she was the wrong sister? Realised too that he'd never checked Stella out at all.

'So…' she said. 'I hope this restaurant is OK

for you. It's one of Stella's favourites.' Adriana looked directly at him, picked up the menu. 'She said to say goodbye as well. She is off to Spain for an extended holiday.'

What? He bit the word back as the ripple of anger returned, threatened to tsunami, and then he saw exactly how tightly Adriana gripped the thick, scripted card. However justified his ire, he would never be guilty of shooting the messenger. So he schooled his features into one of polite interest. 'I wasn't aware that she was planning a holiday.' He put the slightest emphasis on the last word; after all, he'd thought she was planning a wedding.

'It was a last-minute decision. I left her packing up a storm as she's not sure how long she'll be away for. A couple of months at least.'

'I see,' Rob said in a voice that he hoped indicated quite clearly that he didn't.

'Is Spain somewhere you would like to go?' The words stumbled out and he sensed her rising anxiety. 'I mean, not now obviously,' she added.

'Obviously,' he said, realised he'd infused the word with sarcasm, saw the tiniest of flinches from Adriana and the quick glance she shot round the room.

Come on, Rob. Pull it together.

There was press nearby and the last thing he wanted to see splashed the next day was *Viscount in Awkward First Date Since Heartbreak and Scandal!* or *Heir to Earldom Reduces Honourable Adriana Morrison to Tears!* He and Stella had been in agreement that their first date had to generate positive spin, be the first step towards good publicity for them both. 'Because right now I'm here with you and there's nowhere I'd rather be.'

Adriana looked as though she wanted to flinch again in defence against the sheer cheesiness he'd uttered. 'How sweet,' she said softly, and this time it was her voice that held a hint of sarcasm, though her smile didn't waver. 'Anyway, Stella sends her best and I'm under strict instructions to tell her how it all goes, seeing as *she* set us up!' So that was the story and he had to admire the way she had manoeuvred the conversation.

Before he could respond the maître d' approached. 'The champagne, as ordered.'

Rob glanced at Adriana, saw her ever so slight nod of the head, knew it meant that Stella had primed her for this bit of the date. 'How lovely,' she said as the cork was expertly popped and the amber liquid poured into the delicate crystal flutes.

He lifted his glass. 'What shall we drink to?'

'New beginnings,' she said, exactly as scripted by Stella, but then added in an undertone, 'Wherever they take us.'

As they clinked Rob was aware of the woman at the next table taking a photograph, ostensibly of her table, but he had little doubt that the real target was them. Stella's journalist, no doubt. In the aftermath Adriana leant forward. 'Sorry,' she whispered as she rose from the table. 'I need to pop to the loo.'

Rob watched as she walked away, one hundred per cent sure that the apology had not been because she needed a bathroom break, but for this whole situation. So in the space of ten minutes Adriana had managed to apologise, let him know that Stella was absconding to Spain and that the new story for this date was that it was a set-up. Later he'd demand an explanation but for now he had no wish to generate negative publicity, so he'd go along with it—if the Honourable Adriana wanted a first date, damn it, he'd give her one.

CHAPTER TWO

ADRIANA RESISTED THE urge to rest her forehead against the cool of the mirror, all too aware that right now there was every chance she was being watched. She knew exactly what lengths the press would go to for a picture, so she knew better than to let her guard drop even in the supposed privacy of the restaurant bathroom. But she did need a few moments to pull herself together, even if it was just to get her hormones under control. Because, mortifying though it was, the second she had seen Viscount Rochester her hormones had stood to attention. Not helped by her stupid stumble into his arms; Adriana glanced down at her unaccustomedly high heels with loathing.

The only saving grace was that if he had clocked her awareness of him she could put it down to her acting skills. Because they needed to make this date believable—she could only hope she'd got that message across.

The last thing any of them needed was some enterprising journalist putting two and two together, wondering why Stella had pulled out at the last minute and figuring out the truth. So somehow she had to make this look good. The question was, how? She had no idea how to flirt or hold witty conversations or play to the press. That was Stella's domain—by now she would have dazzled Rob, captivated him, had him halfway on the road to falling in love with her. Even though that wasn't part of the plan, Stella had always been very clear that she had no interest in love, yet such was her charm that men fell for her like proverbial ninepins, dazzled, lured, captivated.

Adriana glanced at her reflection and sighed. Stella had certain assets that she quite simply lacked. Glossy corn-blonde hair that never ever frizzed, sparkling blue eyes framed by impossibly long lashes, delicate features, and a figure that wouldn't look out of place on the catwalk.

Adriana, on the other hand—genetics had graced her with light-brown hair that had got more than a fair share of frizz factor. Her grey eyes were her best feature but her eyelashes were too light, her nose too 'aristocratic', in other words too large, and her mouth a tad too generous. Average height, average figure…average—that was what she was. No one would ever give her a second glance when Stella was in the room.

Enough. Stella wasn't in the room and Adriana would not let her sister down, would not be the one responsible for unleashing another scandal on the family. All she had to do was make one date look *believable*; it didn't have to look successful.

Picking up her bag, she returned to the restaurant, paused for an instant as her gaze lingered on Rob. And there it was, the thing that was making this 'date' even worse. The stupid little lurch in her tummy, the hardly acknowledged tiny wish that this was a real date.

Then again, it wasn't surprising—by anyone's standards he was gorgeous. Thick blonde hair, dark blue eyes, and the craggy good looks that could easily grace the silver screen. Tall, broad-shouldered, lithely muscled and…so far out of Adriana's league she may as well live on a different planet.

Yet for the next hour or so she had to make this look real. A quick glance at the table next to them showed her that the woman who had been taking photos was still there and unless

Adriana was imagining it she had inched her chair round the table so she was closer to Rob. No doubt her plan was to have a go at either recording their conversation or indulging in some good old-fashioned eavesdropping.

So as she sat down she smiled, picked up the champagne and sipped it, resisted the temptation to gulp the bubbles down. Tried not to focus on the shape of his forearm as he reached for his own glass, tried not to focus too much on the deep blue of his eyes, or the slight unruliness of his hair or…

Aaargh!

She stared down at the menu. 'Have you decided what to have?'

'I thought I'd have the lamb. What about you?'

She studied the menu. 'Hmm. Stella always says…' She broke off. What was wrong with her? Why on earth would she bring up Stella? Probably because she had no doubt at all that Rob was thinking about Stella. Just like Steve…her one serious boyfriend, the one man she'd believed preferred her to her sister, had turned out to be a crackpot, a secret stalker who had fabricated a whole relationship with Adriana to be nearer to Stella. You couldn't write the script. But unfortunately it hadn't been fiction and her skin still crawled when she remembered Steve. Recalled finding his cache of press clipping about Stella, the pictures on the wall, his secret shrine to her sister and worst of all his diary—that described his feelings for Stella. He hadn't even denied it when she'd confronted him, had expected her to understand and accept how he felt, to feel grateful for his attention.

'I know I am not worthy of her, but at least through you I feel closer to her.'

She'd felt such a fool, felt as though no shower, no body scrub would wash away the mortification—because for a few stupid months she'd allowed herself to believe that someone loved her for her. Preferred her to Stella. She should have learnt from her father that she wasn't worthy of love, could never be equal to, let alone better than Stella. It was a lesson she wouldn't forget again.

'What does Stella always say?'

Sensing that this wasn't the first time he'd asked, she pulled herself together. 'Not to have salad on a first date in case you get spinach stuck in your teeth. And to avoid linguini or spaghetti or you'll spend more time on working out how to eat it properly than you will listening to your date.'

'Are there any other rules I should know? I am guessing soup is out—in case you slurp it by mistake.' She glanced up at him, saw that he had relaxed, could see amusement in his eyes, and as for his smile…she was pretty sure her toes were curling in her despised high heels. Some tension drained away; it looked as though Rob was going to play along.

'That's true.' She considered for a moment. 'And I suppose garlic is only OK if you both eat it.' Adriana broke off as heat touched her cheeks. 'I mean…in case you end up driving home together.' Fabulous. She'd made it worse. Defiantly she stuck her chin out. In for a penny, in for a pound. 'But FYI one of my rules is no kissing on a first date. So you can order extra garlic if you want.'

Now his gaze lingered on her lips and she'd swear they tingled. '*I* always think rules are made to be broken,' he said softly.

She stared at him, her senses suddenly awhirl even as she reminded herself this was all a show for the cameras. 'In that case I'd better order linguine with a side of salad.' She smiled. 'But I'll avoid garlic. Just in case.'

His smile morphed into a grin. 'Or how about this? Let's both order exactly what we want. But we'll make a deal. I'll tell you if you have spinach in your teeth and vice versa. Deal?' He held out his hand.

'Deal,' she said, told herself it was a simple handshake as she placed her hand in his.

But there was nothing simple about the feel of his skin against hers; logic told her electric shocks were the stuff of myths but no way was the tingle that ran up her arm a figment of her imagination. Her startled glance met his and she was almost sure his reaction matched hers.

Almost.

'Right. In all seriousness, I'll have the lamb as well. There's nothing worse than staring at someone else's plate wishing you could have their food.'

'Is that another first-date etiquette thing?'

'Nope. That's just me.' And she knew why. When she was a child, if they went out for dinner as a family and she couldn't be left behind her father made a point of allowing Stella to order whatever she liked and getting Adriana the cheapest thing on the menu. The same principle had run through the whole of her upbringing—only the best for Stella, only the worst for Adriana. In the end Adriana had accepted it as her lot.

Rob looked as though he was waiting for an

explanation and it was a relief when the waiter arrived to take the order.

'I'll have the leg of lamb with salsa verde, please.'

'Same for me. Thank you.'

'Of course,' the waiter said. 'And perhaps you would like the chef's special recommendation with that? Wild garlic fondant potatoes?'

Adriana glanced at Rob and saw a glimmer of amusement light his eyes, and she couldn't help it. 'That sounds divine,' she said. 'Yes, please.'

'Then the same for me as well,' he said.

Once the waiter had gone he leant back and picked up his champagne. 'To garlic,' he said. 'And breaking the rules.'

As she met his gaze she could feel desire melt over her skin at the huskiness of his voice. The clink of the glasses somehow momentous as though the echo reverberated.

'I… That reminds me of a joke,' she said hurriedly. 'What does garlic do when it's hot?'

He considered, then, 'I give up. What does it do?'

Too late she remembered the punchline, wished her brain hadn't scrambled. 'Takes its cloves off.'

There was a silence and he chuckled. 'I like it,' he said.

And then she was laughing too at the sheer inanity of it.

'Though I do wonder what brought that particular joke to mind.' His words were deep and flirtatious and teasing and they caused a breathless gasp to fall from her lips.

'It's the only joke I know about garlic,' she said with as much dignity as she could muster, and he chuckled again.

'Touché. Though I could come up with a few about taking one's clothes off.' With that he wiggled his eyebrows and she full-on laughed.

'I'll pass, thank you.'

'Probably wise. But on a serious note, tell me how you've been. Do you still not like parties?'

'Oh.' Surprise and a funny sense of warmth touched her. 'You remember. And no, I still don't, but now I can choose not to go. Though if I do I still end up tidying up. What about you? Are you still the King of the Wooden Blocks?'

'I haven't tried my hand at that for a while.' He sipped his drink. 'I also remember that you said you were hoping to start work on your father's estate. Did you do that?'

She paused as the waiter arrived with the food, smiled her thanks and sampled a first mouthful before replying.

'Yes, I did.' She'd always known that Salvington was destined for Stella, that that was Plan A and Plan C. It had never even occurred to her father to have a Plan D that involved Adriana, even though Salvington could be safeguarded if Adriana had a son. In truth she believed her father would prefer for Salvington to go to a distant relative, rather than risk a son of Adriana's becoming heir.

But it didn't stop her from loving Salvington with a deep, instinctive love, her connection to her home an invisible thread that linked her to the woodland, the farmland, the earth, the sheer majestic beauty of the place, steeped in history.

Perhaps that link had been forged in childhood, when, in her quest to be invisible, she'd spent hours and hours wandering and exploring the acres of fields and country, the woods and stables. Knew every inch, every nook and cranny, had spent hours looking at wildlife, inspecting the soil, climbing the trees. When she was older she'd taken a sketchbook with her, capturing different bits of the estate on paper, with pencils and charcoal. Sketches she'd later try and paint in the privacy of a seldom-used room she'd turned into her 'study'. It had been a form of escape, even if in some ways it had compounded her guilt, that all this may be lost because of her.

She could only hope that the law would be changed or that Plan C would work and Stella would provide an heir. If that happened then one day Adriana could become estate manager, if not whilst her father was alive then at some point in the future.

But Adriana knew that plans changed, that this may be her only chance to work on the land she loved. So she'd summoned up the courage to suggest to her father that she could help, and he'd agreed, though his consent couldn't be classed as gracious.

'I suppose the least you can do is try to earn your board and food.'

'Do you enjoy it?' Rob asked.

'Yes, I do. I really do. Though sometimes it's a bit frustrating.' She broke off, suddenly aware how easy their conversation had become—he'd had the ability to make a shy twenty-year-old hold a conversation and clearly he still did.

'Why is that? I'd really like to know. Seeing

as I am about to take over running the Darrow estate from my father.'

Envy touched her as she tried to imagine what that must feel like, to be able to say those words. 'These aren't the type of frustrations you'll have. You'll have free rein.'

'So you have ideas you'd like to implement but you aren't allowed to?' His tone was puzzled. 'If they are good ideas surely your father would be happy to consider them.'

It was hard to keep the snort from escaping. For a start her father belittled every idea she had on principle. But to be fair there were other considerations as well. 'Not really,' she explained. 'He feels there is no point in making innovations if the estate ends up in the hands of the current heir, who is more than likely to sell it and doesn't care if it turned into a golf course or an industrial park. So he thinks any innovations should be up to Stella once she is married and has a son.' She broke off. Why, oh, why was she so gauche? Everything had been going so well but those words had plummeted lead-balloon-like into the atmosphere.

He picked up his glass, a frown furrowing his forehead. 'So in some ways Stella getting married would be…problematic for you. It would be hard for you to see Stella step in, take over, be allowed to implement innovations.' His blue eyes had narrowed slightly and Adriana could almost see the cogs whir in his brain as though he suspected she'd somehow sabotaged his plans with Stella.

'Absolutely not.' And in any case she knew one day Stella would listen to her ideas, would implement them. But that was the sisters' secret. 'I want what is right for Salvington and that is for Stella to get married and have a son.' She kept her voice low and a smile on her face, aware of the nearby journalists. 'My love for Salvington means I will happily step aside knowing it will stay in the family. So when Stella marries my plan is to go forth and have a life of adventure—I'll go travelling, maybe help run a cattle ranch in Australia or work on a vineyard in the South of France. The world will be my oyster.' In truth these plans were less than completely formulated, but they held good. As a stop gap. 'I want Stella to get married sooner rather than later. Because once she has a son Salvington is completely safe.'

Really, Adriana? Worse and worse—this was not the way she wanted the conversation to go at all. A hint of anger showed in the twist of his lips and she couldn't blame him. After all, he'd believed he was going to marry Stella within weeks.

His expression still hard, he nodded. 'Understood.' She finished her last mouthful, saw that he'd also finished eating, had pushed his plate away. Knew that the mention of Stella had reminded them both of why they were here. 'I've got an idea. How about we go somewhere else for dessert? Somewhere more private,' he added. The smile was back in place, the charm-filled tone of his voice sounding like a man on a first date suggesting a dalliance. But this time his smile didn't reach his eyes and Adriana felt a little lurch of trepidation. It was time to face the music, explain the reason for Stella's no-show in more detail. A conversation she was not going to enjoy. This may not be her fault, but life had taught her that facts were irrelevant. Rob had the right to be upset but she couldn't help wishing she wasn't the one in the line of fire. But as his date she was presumably supposed to look pleased at the suggestion.

'Oh…um…yes. That sounds…lovely,' she managed. 'How about we go for a walk in the park? We could get hot chocolate and cake.' It probably wasn't what he had in mind but at least she was pretty sure he wouldn't lose his temper in a public place. So they would have a civilised conversation and then go their separate ways. It would be fine. Though as she glanced at the clench of his determined jaw, trepidation touched her anew.

CHAPTER THREE

ROB STRODE TOWARDS the open spaces of the park. At least he would now get some straight answers. The past hour had been confusing to say the least. He still had no idea why Stella was absconding to Spain and even less idea why that had necessitated Adriana taking her place. Could Adriana have sabotaged the wedding plan in order to keep her job? That seemed far-fetched. Or was it? He glanced down at his companion; her hands shoved in her jacket pocket, she looked distinctly nervous.

Because she was about to be found out? Or perhaps because he was marching along like a man about to go into battle. Forcing himself to slow down, he said, 'I'm pretty sure no one has followed us but let's grab some hot chocolate, double-check we're unaccompanied and then we can talk.'

Adriana nodded. 'Sure.'

Five minutes later, cups in hand, they strolled down a wide, tree-lined pathway. 'OK. So now we can talk. Or rather you can,' he said. 'What is going on? Where is Stella?'

'She really is going to Spain.' Adriana's voice was quiet. 'I'm sorry, Rob, and so is Stella. Truly. But she has changed her mind. She can't…doesn't want to go through with it.'

The words seemed to ricochet through the air, carried back memories of another woman. Of Emily, who had never said those words to his face, but her actions behind his back had screamed the truth loud and clear.

'Can I ask why she has changed her mind?'

'She has feelings for someone else and she doesn't think it's fair to you to go ahead.'

Brilliant. History truly on repeat. Feelings for someone else. Exactly like Emily, only in Emily's case she'd acted on those feelings and had been caught on camera.

Perhaps he should be grateful Stella hadn't done that, but…

'Why didn't she tell me herself? Cancel the date? What was the *point* of that whole charade?' Adriana flinched, looked away, and he thought she wouldn't answer. Then she turned, her face slightly pale.

'She was planning on going through with

it until the very last minute. By the time she changed her mind you would most likely have been in the restaurant—she didn't want you to be captured on camera being stood up. So we thought if I came along the press would hopefully think it was always meant to be me. Unlikely but just about possible.'

Curiosity surfaced through the sensation of ire and disbelief. Why was it unlikely?

'So now all we have to do is fade away—say the date didn't work.'

Only oddly enough it had; a memory of that frisson when they'd touched hands, of the ease of conversation once they'd overcome the initial awkwardness, hit him. The sound of her laughter. All fake, he reminded himself, all done for the sake of the press.

'But please believe that Stella entered your agreement in good faith, she's just been... blindsided.'

He shook his head. 'Blindsided by love. I hope it works out for her.'

'You don't sound like you think it will.'

'I'm not a great believer in love. That's why I'm on the market for an arranged marriage. I thought Stella agreed with me. That love, lust...those are transient feelings. I was offering her certainty, a future that could be relied on.' He could hear the bitterness in his voice.

'You had feelings for her?'

The words made him pause. 'I liked her but I suppose that's the beauty of an arranged marriage—it is a business arrangement first and foremost. So I am upset in the same way I would be if a deal fell through. It's an...'

'Inconvenience?' she offered. 'And you'll be looking for a new partner forthwith?'

'Yes.' Aware that she was looking at him oddly, he said, 'Look, I realise that sounds...'

'Insulting?' Now there was a definite spark to her grey eyes, her lips pressed together in obvious annoyance, and his gaze snagged on her mouth. 'I understand this wasn't a love match but... Stella is a person, not a convenience.'

'I understand that. But we planned a marriage of convenience. So her pulling out is by definition inconvenient.'

'In the same way as a supplier letting you down when you need the parts to manufacture an order?' she asked. 'In which case I'm sure you won't have any problem finding a host of replacements for Stella—a veritable conveyor belt, in fact. You're rich, young, good-looking and you're heir to an earldom. I'd imagine you have women falling all over you.'

There it was again—a flash of how it had felt earlier when she'd literally stumbled into his arms.

He blinked, focused on what she'd said, stung by the slightly derisory tone to her voice. 'It's not that easy. Because if you are going to carry this analogy on, Stella was a rare part, hard to find.' How many women could he trust not to be taking him for a ride, taken in by the glamour and wealth as Emily had been? How many women would genuinely be happy without love? Understand the duty that lay behind being the Countess of Darrow, the commitment to the land, the commitment to staying married, because the alternative was unacceptable, a divorce with the heir not brought up on the estate?

'Of course she was,' Adriana said quietly, and now her voice had lost its tartness, held an understanding. 'And yes, it *will* be hard to replace her—I wish you luck in your search. I will leave you to concoct something for the press if they show any interest in why we aren't taking things further.' She gave a half-laugh. 'You could say I don't fit your business model. Or blame the garlic.'

'Or…' They could go on a second date. The idea came from nowhere. Ridiculous—Adriana was not on the market for a marriage of convenience, whereas he and Stella had been and that made another date redundant, however attractive the idea of putting the garlic theory to the test was. Even more ridiculous. 'I'll come up with something. In the meantime, thank you for saving me the embarrassment of being stood up.'

'No problem.' She hesitated and took a step closer, stood on tiptoe and brushed her lips against his cheek, evoked a scent of jasmine and chocolate and warmth and, oh, how he wanted to prolong the contact. 'Goodbye, Rob.'

'Goodbye.' As she walked away he raised a hand to his cheek, dropped it and turned to walk away.

Adriana climbed out of the taxi and thanked the driver, looked up at the sprawling yet elegant proportions of Salvington Manor. The stone-façade house exuded splendour and history and as always Adriana felt that sense of connection to the edifice that had housed her family for so many generations.

She took a deep breath as she approached the curving arch of the front door—she had heard nothing from Stella and hadn't dared contact her in case she was talking with their father. A call or message from Adriana would do nothing but exacerbate his anger.

She pushed her key into the door and entered as softly as possible. Wanted at all costs to avoid her father. Took her shoes off and held them in one hand and walked quietly along the parquet floor of the hallway, paused suddenly, her senses alert, though she wasn't sure why. Could she hear her mother crying? A distinct possibility if her father had delivered one of his shattering tirades to his wife.

Not for the first time she wondered how it had come to this, recalled her parents' wedding photos, the love shining in their eyes. Followed by a stream of happy photos, the honeymoon, her mother's first pregnancy, Stella's birth, pictures that showed love and laughter and happiness.

Then the stream had dried up with Adriana's arrival. She had been the cause, the catalyst, the turning point that had turned her father into a bitter, vitriolic man, her mother a mass of nerves and misery, Stella still loved but bearing a burden of duty too heavy to carry.

It was then that she saw the figure crumpled at the bottom of the stairs.

Saw that it was the prone figure of her father.

She ran forward, knelt by his side and, fingers fumbling in her haste, she managed to pull her phone out to dial the emergency services.

The next day Stella twisted her hands together as she paced the plush carpet of the lounge of Salvington Manor. 'Oh, God, this is all my fault.'

Adriana shook her head. 'No, Stella, it isn't.'

'It is. When I told him I was pregnant he completely lost it, Ria. He smashed my phone, he shouted, screamed such awful things and told me to get out.'

'Then he yelled at Mum, then he shut himself away with a bottle and then he must have realised something was wrong and got to the stairs. None of that is your fault. The doctor says he believes he has probably had a minor heart attack in the past as well.' Adriana took a deep breath. 'Now they will put in a stent and hopefully he will recover.'

'What if he doesn't?' Stella asked. 'Then Salvington will be lost and it *will* all be my fault.'

'No. It isn't anyone's fault. Unless you want to blame the stupid laws that mean a daughter cannot inherit.' They could not let an archaic, outmoded, outdated system take their land. 'Stella, the father of your baby—is there any way you can marry him, make the baby legitimate? Even if you divorce again once the baby is born?'

Her sister shook her head, eyes wide in her pale face. 'I'm sorry, Ria, but it's not possible. I can't explain but it's not possible. He's…'

'Married already?'

'No. He's engaged to someone else and he's…very high profile. It was a mistake. I just never thought it was possible for me to feel like that, that attracted to any man.'

'Not even Rob?' The words were out before she could call them back. 'Sorry, Stell. That is none of my business.'

'No, not even Rob. I mean, I can see that he is a good-looking man, but I didn't feel it, I just didn't think it mattered. But with… the baby's father it was all-consuming. The slightest touch and there really was some sort of reaction, a spark, an ignition…anyway… none of *that* matters now.' Another twist of her hands.

'No, it doesn't,' Adriana agreed. 'The bottom line is we need a legitimate baby boy and the sooner the better. The doctors have said with care there is no reason for Father not to recover well, but obviously they can't guarantee that and equally obviously he may not take care. So I need to do something.'

'Such as?'

'I've got an idea. I'm not sure if it will work but I have to give it a try. I'm going out. Call me if there is any news from the hospital.'

'But...'

'I promise I'll explain when I get back.'

As she climbed into the family estate car Adriana wondered if she'd completely lost the plot. Perhaps, but all that burned in her was a determination to save Salvington; in her mind images streamed of bulldozers razing the manor to the ground, diggers pulling up the soil with no care for the generations past who had cultivated and loved it. The loss for the local wildlife. She shuddered.

The thoughts churned through her mind as the car covered the miles to the Darrow estate. She wouldn't, couldn't let that happen.

She drove up the wide gravelled driveway without pause; she wouldn't stop now, wouldn't let any doubt cloud her actions, prevent her from this path. Carefully she parked next to the row of cars and went up to the front door, knocked on the ornate knocker shaped like a lion. Her mind took in the detail of the mane, the fierce expression that almost looked as if it was warning her off.

The door was pulled open and she blinked as she took in the majestic form of a butler—she hadn't realised that Rob's family still maintained a high level of staff.

'Hello. I'd like to see Rob...um... Viscount Rochester. It's urgent. I am Adriana Morrison.' She glanced down at herself and then rummaged in her bag. 'I've probably got my driving licence somewhere or...'

'That won't be necessary. I recognise you. Please come this way. Viscount Rochester is in his study. If you will wait in the drawing room I will get him.'

Left in the massive environs of the drawing room, Adriana glanced round, tried to focus on the interior to keep the growing doubts at bay, but the dark red velvet curtains, the heavy antique furniture with brocaded seat covers, the imposing sideboard all intimidated her, and she was convinced the portraits on the panelled oak walls were looking at her in disapproval. Realised it wasn't only Rob's ancestors who disapproved—so too would her father. She knew that her father would hate the idea of her being Salvington's saviour, but circumstances meant he no longer had the luxury of that opinion.

Then the door swung open and Rob entered. As she took in the broadness of his chest, the width of his shoulders, the craggy features Adriana gulped, the enormity of what she was about to do hitting her. If only he didn't have such an impact on her, an impact almost made worse by Stella's description of her mystery man. Because right now she could not afford to be distracted by attraction. This was a business proposal—that was what he wanted— a manufactured marriage constructed on the blocks of convenience. That was what she was here to offer.

Hands outstretched, he approached her and she stepped backwards, knew she couldn't risk touching him, however much she wanted to.

'Adriana, I am so sorry to hear about your father. I was going to call but I didn't want to intrude. I was also worried that it was the situation with Stella that may have triggered his attack and I wasn't sure if my call would be welcome. How is he?'

'He is stable. They are going to put a stent in and they think with proper care he should recover and hopefully not have another attack. As for what caused it, there is no point in speculation. Anyway, that's not why I'm here.'

'Of course not.' He studied her face. 'So why are you here? If I can help in any way of course I will.' He hesitated. 'But I won't marry Stella. If that's what you are here to suggest. Whilst I am sorry for what has happened, that wouldn't be right.'

'I know. That's not why I am here either. I…' All her carefully rehearsed speeches vanished clear out of her head. 'I want you to marry me instead. I'm proposing a merger.'

CHAPTER FOUR

ADRIANA'S WORDS TOOK a while to register in his brain. 'Marry *you* instead,' he echoed, just to be absolutely clear he'd got it right.

'Yes. I know I am not what you wanted. I know I am not Stella. I get she was a rare find and I won't tick as many boxes. But I still think I can fit your business model.' Her voice held an edge of desperation under the calm tone of her voice and he could see the tension in the set of her shoulder, the clench of her delicate jaw.

'Whoa.' Rob raised his hand. 'This is a highly emotional time for you; it is not the right time to make a decision of that magnitude.'

She inhaled deeply, made a visible effort to pull herself together as she nodded acknowledgement. 'I understand that and in different circumstances I would agree with you. But time is of the essence. So would you at least discuss the possibility?'

This would be the moment to shut this conversation down; but…somehow the idea had started to circulate in his brain, to put out a few tendrils of curiosity. And…he couldn't simply send her away—she looked exhausted, her skin pale, her brown hair tangled, and as she pushed her fringe back he could see the strain in her grey eyes. He was tempted to move over and hug her, reminded himself they were barely acquainted, had clocked too her reluctance to take his outstretched hands. But there was something he could do.

'Of course we can talk,' he said. 'But first you need to sit down and I will get us something to eat. Wait here.'

'No…really…'

'I insist. And you may as well eat whilst we talk.'

'Then thank you.'

Ten minutes later he handed her the tray and watched as she selected a sandwich and bit into it.

'Thank you. I hadn't even realised I was hungry—I haven't eaten anything since our lunch yesterday.' Two sandwiches and a mini Scotch egg later she put her plate down and said, 'So... I realise my idea is a bit out of the blue.'

'It is,' he agreed. 'Yesterday you thought the whole idea of replacing Stella quickly was incongruous. You mentioned conveyor belts.'

'I did. And I realise it's a bit rich me climbing aboard the conveyer belt I was so derisive about. But circumstances have changed. Of course I hope and pray that my father makes a full recovery and lives for many more years, but there is no guarantee of that. Yesterday it was important there be a male heir, now it is imperative.'

'Perhaps Stella will marry the new love in her life.'

There was a heartbeat of a hesitation and then, 'It's not that easy—she has feelings for someone. There's a long way to go from that to marrying someone and having a baby. It takes time. And even if that did happen instantly the baby may be a girl. It makes sense to double our chances. For me to get married too.'

'Just like that?' he asked. 'You're willing to change your whole life on a—?'

'Whim?' Her grey eyes sparked with ire. 'Do you of all people believe this to be a whim? Don't you understand what it would mean to lose Salvington? To watch my home torn down, our land desecrated?' There was no denying the depth of her emotions. 'Wouldn't you do anything to save Darrow from that fate?'

Of course he would—duty was the bedrock of his existence, imbued in him since he'd taken his very first breath...hell, before that in all likelihood. Darrow was bred in his blood and bones. And he would do anything to save it.

But it was different for Adriana. 'Yes, I would. But our marriage wouldn't necessarily save Salvington. We may have a girl, or not have a child in time. Plus, if Stella does marry and have a boy in time you would have sacrificed yourself for nothing.'

'I understand that, but I cannot sit back and *do* nothing.' The set of her lips, the twist of her hands spoke of her sincerity. 'There is a chance that Stella won't do that, there is a chance I will have a boy, and once I have a boy Salvington is safe.'

Rob continued to look troubled, though he said nothing more.

Adriana leant forward, her fists clenched. 'I love Salvington and the risk is worth it to me. I want my children to have the chance to explore the land and places that I roamed as a child. I want to keep Salvington in the Morrison family, to see it prosper and grow. I want to be part of that. I will do anything I can do to make that happen.'

'Including having a loveless marriage of convenience?'

She waved her hand in dismissal. 'Love is overrated.'

Whilst he agreed whole-heartedly, he reminded her that, 'Those are words. Similar to those that Stella said, and she changed her mind.'

'That wouldn't happen with me.'

'You can't know that.' After all, he'd taken Stella's words at their face value, blithely accepted that she held the same beliefs about marriage as he did, sure that what he had to offer was acceptable. With hindsight he could see now how foolish that was, that he should have probed and questioned. 'Most people want to fall in love, to love and be loved, to have the happy-ever-after.'

'I don't.'

'Why not?'

'I don't see why my reasons matter. They are personal.'

'Marriage is personal.'

That drew a reluctant smile from her, and

as his gaze snagged on the upturn of her lips he felt it again, that insidious dart of desire. 'Fair enough. I get you need an explanation. I am sure you know from the press how tumultuous my parents' marriage has been—yet once they loved each other. I've witnessed that roller coaster and I'd rather avoid it. Love doesn't last.'

'Your parents are one example of love gone wrong. I am sure you could cite plenty of examples of happier marriages where love did last.'

'Of course, and I don't believe all relationships based on love are doomed. But I do know that for me personally it isn't worth the risk.'

'Just because of your parents?'

'No. That is a big factor but there is more than that. I did take the risk once and it didn't work out. I loved him, I thought he loved me, turned out he didn't. I will not put myself through that again. Love made me blind and stupid. Left me hurt and exhausted. I would rather live in calm and peace, be my own person.'

He blinked—he couldn't have put it better himself. 'I get that. I am sure you know of my previous ill-fated matrimonial venture.' You'd have had to live on Mars to miss the publicity.

'I know you had a very public break-up, but I didn't read the detail. I avoid stories like that wherever I can.'

'It wasn't pretty and I have no wish to repeat it. So I am not offering or expecting love.' He hesitated. 'But I do want a life-long commitment. Our child would be heir to the Darrow estate; would need to live here, be brought up here.' That was an absolute, though a part of him apologised in advance to this potential child, whose fate was already being written before he or she had even been conceived.

'I understand that.'

The words were quick, too quick, and he shook his head. 'I'm not sure you do, or rather I am not sure you really do. You are thinking about the here and now, your present need.' His eyes narrowed. 'I am not just a temporary convenience, this is a marriage of convenience, and that means thinking about the future, the rest of your life. You cannot give birth to a son, then discover that our marriage has become "inconvenient" and take him off to Salvington. Neither can you give birth to a girl and decide to take her away from her birthright.' Darrow was one of the few peerages in England that allowed descent through the female line, so his first child regardless of sex would inherit.

'I wouldn't do that.' She hesitated. 'Though if our son does end up inheriting Salvington then we would have to work something out. I would want him to grow up knowing Salvington too, so we would maybe have to live some of the time at Salvington. But of course I wouldn't take him away from Darrow.'

'No, you wouldn't,' he agreed. 'I would ask you to do as Stella agreed. Sign a prenup that states if you instigate a divorce I get custody.'

'And Stella agreed to that?' He could hear incredulity in her voice and then she rolled her eyes with a muttered, 'Of course she did.'

'Yes, she did. She was sure there would be no question of divorce. So it made sense. Just as we both agreed to have a full health check before the wedding.' Another thing that made sense.

'Well, I am not Stella. I wouldn't sign something that gives you carte blanche to behave however badly you want, all the while knowing I couldn't leave you without losing my child.'

He raised his eyebrows as annoyance rasped. 'That's rather an insulting assumption. That I would *wish* to behave like that.'

'It's an equally insulting assumption to think I would take our baby and run,' she snapped.

They glared at each other and it occurred to

Rob that when he and Stella had come to their agreement there had been no sparring, no arguments; instead there had been quiet, calm negotiation. He inhaled deeply. 'OK. Let's take a step back. I wasn't trying to insult you—I was trying to point out that you haven't thought this through. I have.'

'On the contrary, I'm thinking very clearly about an element of your plan that could prove hugely detrimental to me and our children.'

Rob frowned, trying to damp down the anger she provoked in him. Realised that part of that anger was because Adriana was in fact correct, and yet a sense of outrage remained that she would even consider that he would behave in an abusive way. Do anything detrimental to his children. Yet logically she did have a valid point, and using logic was paramount here.

'OK. Point accepted.' He did his best to keep the tightness from his voice. 'We could word the prenup in a way that protects us both. So in the case of my being abusive, or whatever you are envisaging in this carte blanche behaviour, then I wouldn't get sole custody.'

'That would work for me.'

Whoa. How had the conversation moved so fast? And why had he let emotion in? Emotion clouded logic, got in the way of a properly negotiated, mutually beneficial agreement that would lead to a calm, well-oiled marriage that would leave him free to do his duty by the estate *and* take on a proper role in Easel. So the sooner he got the marriage box ticked the better, but only to the right woman. One who fulfilled all the necessary criteria. And he wasn't at all sure Adriana did that.

'Hold on. That was a strictly hypothetical scenario. I have a whole heap of concerns about this idea. I won't take advantage of your situation. You are grieving and scared and worried—you can't commit the rest of your life on the off chance it may save Salvington.' Plus, Adriana had spoken of travel, of adventure. He wouldn't marry someone who would regret it, wouldn't let her give up her dreams.

'Yes, I can. That is my decision, my choice to make. You are willing to marry for duty's sake. You were willing to marry Stella when she was marrying for duty's sake. So what is the problem?'

He opened his mouth to explain, but before he could speak her expression changed. She shook her head and rose to her feet. 'It's OK. You don't have to answer that. I'm sorry. You're right. This is a stupid idea. I apologise for disturbing you. Thank you for the sand-wiches.'

Huh? Confusion froze him to his chair as he tried to figure out what had caused the volte face. Swore he saw hurt flash across her grey eyes, saw the lips he'd tried so hard not to dwell on tremble before setting in a line. What was going on here? And did it matter? It made sense to let her go—after all, it was a daft idea. Yet…he didn't want to, not like this. Not if she was upset, when she was already worried about her father and the future. 'Adriana. Wait.'

Adriana didn't want to wait—could still feel mortification roil inside her. She was an idiot. Rob had been planning on marrying Stella. That was hardly much of a sacrifice. So, yes, he wanted a marriage of convenience, but there was a big difference between a convenient marriage with Stella and a convenient marriage with Adriana.

Rob was not in her league and she had been a fool to come here. He'd even told her Stella had been a rare find and yet she'd waltzed in here, offering herself as a substitute. What had she been thinking?

Clearly she hadn't or perhaps, most mortifying of all, she had been acting on the vestiges of her own stupid crush on him, on the pull of attraction that she couldn't shift. Even now. As she reluctantly turned to face him, still she noticed his looks, his stance, the strength of him. But she wouldn't show it, somehow she had to retreat with dignity. Forcing a small smile to her lips, she said lightly, 'Really. There is no need for further discussion. I'd be grateful if you forgot this whole conversation.'

'I don't think that's possible.' He studied her expression and she forced herself to meet the dark blue gaze. 'And I want to answer your question. Tell you why, if I was going to marry Stella, I have a problem with your proposal.'

She didn't need an answer, certainly didn't need to listen to a litany of her sister's many virtues. Better if she got in first. 'You don't have to explain. I get it. Stella is beautiful, witty, and she is perfect countess material. I know that—and I know I'm not.'

'What?' Rob looked genuinely confused. 'That's not what I was going to say at all. I mean, yes, Stella is all those things, but that's not the problem. I was going to marry Stella because I believed she wanted a convenient marriage. That she has been brought up to marry for duty, to provide an heir. You weren't and this isn't what you want. Yesterday you told me you want to travel, to run a cattle ranch in Australia, to have an adventure. That is your dream. I can't allow you to give that up for a convenient marriage that may not even achieve its goal.'

She studied his expression, could see nothing but sincerity there, and a small tendril of surprise touched her. 'I understand your reservations. But the ranch, the travel, they weren't my dream. They were a *plan*, something I thought I may enjoy for a while. But they weren't inspired by a yearning or a compulsion.' Not like her art—that was a passion, a necessity, something she loved though would never dare to dream about. 'Travel was more of an idea.' A stopgap. 'Not travelling is not a sacrifice for me, it won't cause me sadness. Standing by and doing nothing to save Salvington—that would devastate me. I know it may be lost anyway but I have to know I tried everything to save it.'

There was a long silence and then he shrugged. 'In that case, here's what I'll offer. Stay for dinner. Let's talk about this more, see if it really is a possibility.'

Relief rocked through her. 'I'd like that.'

'Then come with me. I have a separate annexe that I use when I stay here. I'll get dinner on and we can start talking.' A sudden rush of adrenalin jolted through her, heightened by the enormity of it all, and further still as he rose to his feet and she caught her breath. Was she really about to discuss the idea of marrying this man? Blond hair a touch unruly, his dark eyes held a hint of a smile. 'Call it a preliminary discussion.'

One that she had to focus on, rather than the fluttery feeling in her tummy. A feeling she was going to put down to nerves—would not let it be attraction. Attraction had no place at the table. Look where attraction had got Stella.

She returned his smile with one of her own. 'Bring it on.'

CHAPTER FIVE

ADRIANA FOLLOWED HIM through the grandeur of the hallway and up a massive curving staircase, along a narrow corridor into the annexe.

She liked the area at once; it had a comfortable feel to it. The lounge had a large, overstuffed sofa and two mismatched armchairs. A computer was set up in one corner and there was a flat-screen TV on one wall. The other walls were dotted with pictures and she walked over to look at them.

'I like these,' she said, as she studied the line drawings, deceptively simple yet emotive. Clean and beautiful and expressive.

'So do I. My parents don't think they are grand enough—they prefer the family portraits and landscapes and oils. I found these in the attic—I have no idea who the artist is, they aren't signed, but I like them.'

'Perhaps one of your ancestors drew them,'

she said, liking that idea. Sometimes she wondered if one day one of her own descendants would find her drawings hidden away in an attic and hopefully find something to like in them. 'Anyway, can I help with dinner?'

'As it happens I made a venison stew last time I was here and froze some portions—so it shouldn't take long to rustle that up. We can have bread and I can make a salad to go with it.'

'I'm impressed,' she said. 'You made the casserole.'

'With these very hands.'

She couldn't help herself: she looked down, studied his hands, and for an absurd moment desire melted through her. The shape of his wrist, the length of his fingers all evoked a yearning to feel those hands on her skin, evoked too an urge to draw them, to try and capture their sheer masculine beauty.

'Adriana? You OK?'

'Of course—absolutely.' She could hardly say that she was distracted by his hands, or ask permission to draw them. He'd think she'd lost the plot. Anyway, she didn't tell anyone about her drawings.

She watched as he made a salad, tried not to fixate on the deftness of his movements, the tang of vinegar in the air, the sound of the knife thudding on the chopping board. Every detail seemed seared on her mind, made conversation almost impossible. The sheer intimacy of it all threatened to overwhelm.

Get it together. This was nothing to do with cosy intimacy—this was a working dinner that by necessity needed to be a private one. This was about a need for her to somehow convince Rob that she could be a good choice of bride. Not up to Stella's standard maybe but still a viable choice. Second best, but in truth she had lived with that all her life. The realisation was enough to snap her out of her hormone-induced trance.

'I could set the table if you tell me where everything is.'

Ten minutes later they were sitting at the square wooden table in front of a bay window that overlooked the expanse of a kitchen garden. Adriana gazed out in the gloom of the dusk, tried to gather her thoughts together. 'Maybe you should tell me what your expectations of a marriage are. What you're looking for from a wife.' As she said the words she glanced at him, the way the lighting glinted on his blond hair, the strength of his features, watched the strong column of his throat as he sipped his wine. And all of a sudden her question seemed to take on another meaning, a double entendre she hadn't intended.

His blue eyes studied her and she wondered if he could read her thoughts, wondered whether his own thoughts had taken the same errant turn. But she couldn't wrench her gaze away, couldn't stop looking at him. Her mouth dried and her brain seemed to fuzz as her gaze lingered on his forearms, sleeves rolled up as he ladled a portion of stew onto her plate. The rich aroma almost dizzied her as she took the plate from him. Next her eyes zoned in on the shadow of stubble on his jaw, saw a small scar on the side of his chin, and her fingers tingled with a desire to touch the determined square…

Enough.

Clearing her throat, she somehow forced her vocal cords into compliance. 'Sorry. I got distracted by this delicious meal. Where were we?'

'Our expectations from a marriage,' he drawled, and as his voice melted over her skin she was sure, almost sure, that his eyes had darkened, that he felt the same way she did.

'Why don't you go first?' she said. 'I assume you want someone who will be a good countess.' Her emphasis on the last word would hopefully move this conversation to the proper footing.

He nodded. 'Yes. My mother is on various charitable committees, she also organises the annual fairs on our land and helps with the village fair as well. Then there are various dinners and events.'

All things Stella would have revelled in. And things she would have to learn about. 'My mother will be happy to talk you through what she does. But my wife will have to hit the ground running to a degree as my parents are planning on spending a few months every year in the family villa in Portugal.'

Adriana nodded. 'I understand. Any other expectations?

'No scandal.' He met her gaze fair and square, but now she could see the grim set of his lips, hear the harsh rasp to his voice. 'Both our families have suffered because of the press—I do not want that to happen again. So my wife must behave in such a way that there is not so much as a hint of scandal.'

'I assume that this rule goes for you as well.'

'Of course.'

'But just to be clear, by that do you mean don't get found out or don't engage in any scandalous behaviour?' Heat touched her cheeks.

'I understand that fidelity is a big thing to ask for, but it's important to me...' She'd seen her mother's grief and humiliation first-hand when her father embarked on his affair. As for Adriana herself, the idea that every time Steve touched her he'd been thinking of her sister was an act of unfaithfulness that still made her skin crawl.

'It isn't a big ask.' The words were sharp and she remembered that, whilst she didn't know the details, she did know his fiancée had been unfaithful to him. 'I am asking for fidelity and I intend to return the favour.'

Relief trickled through her, but alongside that was scepticism. It was easy to promise loyalty, and if he'd been marrying Stella she doubted that he would have any issues. But with her...it seemed too much to expect.

'But our marriage will be one of convenience—over the years there will be the temptation to stray.'

'Will there? Are you trying to tell me something? That I won't be enough for you, or that you find me completely unattractive?' There was a glint in his eye, one she couldn't interpret, and his tone was edged. How had she got herself into this conversation and what could she do now? No way would she, could she admit she thought he was drop-dead gorgeous, so she settled for her wooden expression, the one she deployed when she hoped her father would abandon whatever conversation was working him up. The one where she did her best to project invisibility.

He looked at her and exhaled a long sigh, ran a hand through his hair. 'I'm sorry. I don't mean to make you uncomfortable, but Stella and I didn't discuss attraction or fidelity—and it seems clear that we should have. Compatibility is all very well at dinner but it's important in the bedroom as well.'

To her intense annoyance she could feel a blush touch her cheeks. Of course he and Stella hadn't discussed it. Why would they? Stella was infinitely desirable and attractive—so every man in the world would assume compatibility. Anger laced her voice. 'Well, I'm not really sure how we can test that out.'

Now he smiled and it was a smile that made her dizzy with awareness. 'I can think of a few ways.'

Confusion whirled in her head—was he flirting with her? Surely not—he was the one who wanted a business partnership. Yet…as she looked at him all she wanted to do was lean over, grab him by his collar and kiss him.

But she couldn't—damn it, she didn't have the confidence, was too scared that he'd reject her, and so she'd do what she always did. Play it safe. 'Perhaps we should just wait and see how we feel—I mean, attraction doesn't necessarily spring up straight away.'

His withdrawal was instant as his face assumed polite neutrality. 'Of course. You're right. This can wait for another time.' Yet she'd swear that for an instant rue and regret tinged the blue of his eyes as they lingered just a fraction of a second too long on her lips. Had he been thinking about kissing her? Surely not— just her fevered imagination having a wishful think. He rose to his feet.

'I'll get dessert,' he said.

As he stood in the small kitchen, Rob was aware of a disproportionate sense of disappointment—was he really so rusty that he couldn't read the signals? He'd thought there was a spark, been sure of it. Now he wondered if it was wishful thinking. Again. He'd believed Emily had been attracted to him and it had turned out she'd been pretending, acting, faking. So clearly, reading signals was not his forte.

'Rob?'

He turned and saw Adriana standing in the doorway, two plates in hand. 'I thought I could help?'

'Thank you.' But now they were standing there he felt rooted to the spot, mesmerised by how elusive a grey her eyes were, a beautiful, expressive grey, fringed by long lashes, that contrasted with the light-brown of her hair. Hair that held a glossy sheen that begged his fingers to smooth it over. Now that he studied her face he could see the character in the planes and angles, the high bridge of her nose, the shape of her mouth.

'I'll take them.' Aware that his voice sounded rough, he cleared his throat and stepped forward, saw the spark in her eyes, the slight darkening of her pupils, and again he was sure that he was right, that she too felt the pull.

'Sure.' She handed over the plates, and his hand inadvertently brushed against hers. With an audible gasp she stepped backwards and one of the plates crashed to the floor. 'Oh, God. I am so, so sorry. That was so clumsy of me. I'll clear it up and replace it obviously. Is it part of a set? I hope it's not an heirloom or a—'

'Whoa. It's OK. They aren't heirlooms and it was my fault as much as yours. Really, leave it for now. It doesn't matter.'

'It does to me. I hate being clumsy. I'll clear it up. Where is your dustpan and brush?'

'You weren't clumsy.' Though perhaps that was a more palatable explanation than the truth—that the sheer jolt of attraction had caused them both to recoil in shock. Moving away, he opened a cupboard and took out a dustpan and brush, squatted down to brush the pieces up.

'I'll do it.' She dropped down and he forced himself to continue sweeping, not to tense up at her nearness.

'It's fine.' The words were jerky. 'Really. And again I apologise for bringing up the whole attraction factor. It seems to have...derailed negotiations a bit.'

'And I don't want it to do that. That's what I wanted to say really. I completely understand that it will take you a while to adjust to the idea of me rather than Stella. Please don't think I expect you to feel a spark instantly or any time soon.'

Huh? The penny dropped with a clang and he quickly placed the dustpan and brush down, rose, held out a hand and helped her to her feet. 'Adriana, I am an insensitive idiot. But... Stella and I...we never so much as held hands. And it seems clear now why—there was no spark.'

And he'd been so busy outlining all the advantages of a convenient marriage he hadn't even thought about it. If anything he'd been pleased, because after Emily the last thing he wanted were the emotions that attraction could bring.

Her eyes held disbelief. 'I find that difficult to believe. Stella is hardly an antidote.'

'No. Stella is a beautiful woman—I get that, I see that she is attractive, and maybe that's why I didn't really question that side of things. I just assumed...'

'That it would all be all right on the night?' she asked, and he saw the glimmer of a smile.

'Yes. After Emily I was so focused on a marriage of convenience, one without emotional roller coasters, that I didn't see instant attraction as a necessity. I wanted to make decisions based on logic and the long-term, not attraction.'

'And now?' she asked, and her voice was almost a whisper.

'Now...' He looked at her and his breath caught in his throat as desire jolted through him. Warning bells started to clang at the back of his mind. He would not let his decisions be governed by desire, by the magnetic pull of attraction. But, 'Now I can see that perhaps I was wrong not to consider attraction—if Stella and I had discussed it, perhaps we would never have agreed to marry at all. Because attraction is important.'

'But not the be-all and end-all.'

'Agreed. Attraction is a factor but not the most important one.'

Adriana nodded, her gaze not wavering from his. 'And how do we assess the attraction factor?' Her voice was slightly breathless and he wondered what was going through her mind. He could see a pulse beat in her throat and his finger tingled with a need to test her heart rate, check it against his own.

He knew he should back off, but he didn't care, knew that it would be impossible not to kiss her. 'Like this,' he said, and he stepped forward as Adriana did the same.

Then he was kissing her and nothing else mattered except the glorious feel of her lips against his, the scent of her, the taste of her. As he tangled his fingers in the glossy silk of her hair, as he deepened the kiss and heard her small gasp of pleasure, the world spun and he lost himself entirely in the kiss.

Until the ping of the oven recalled them both to the here and now and they both stepped back, stared at each other in mutual shock. 'I…

um…' Adriana visibly pulled herself together. 'I guess that means dessert is ready.'

Rob nodded, even as he urged his vocal cords into action. 'Yes. I'll dish it up. It's just a shop-bought chocolate pudding. I hope that's OK.'

'Absolutely. That sounds perfect.'

The words were forced, meaningless amid the after-effects of desire.

On automatic pilot he found plates and cutlery, noted she made no move to help him. Keeping their distance seemed like the best plan for now, whilst he tried to work out what the hell had happened there. He'd expected a kiss, not a Kiss with a capital K that rated somewhere off the Richter scale.

As they sat down again he cleared his throat. 'I suggest we…'

'Put the kiss firmly behind us. Tick the attraction-factor box and don't let attraction affect our decisions.' The words were said in a rush.

'Exactly.' Though he couldn't help wondering how easy it would be to close Pandora's box. Not when his whole body still strummed and hummed with desire.

'So what now?' she asked.

'You asked me what I expect from a marriage; now I need to know what is important to you.'

The question caught her attention and he could almost see her push away the aftershock of the kiss. She paused to marshal her thoughts, pushed her fringe away from her face in an impatient gesture.

'I need to know you will be a good father. That we will be good parents. Part of the reason we would be entering this agreement is because we both want an heir, but our child needs to be more than that to us. I don't want love for myself. But I would expect our children to have your love.'

'They will.' He kept his voice gentle, not wanting to insult her but knowing this was important. 'Regardless of their sex. But I know that's easy for me to say. We do both want an heir but the heir to Darrow can be a girl or a boy. You need a son to save Salvington. So I am sorry to ask this, but how will you feel if our first child is a girl?'

'I will love my child regardless of its sex, and that is a promise. I will never let my daughter be anything other than loved and cherished. Never feel disappointed in her. I swear it.' Her hands clenched into fists. 'I'm not capable of that.'

He could hear the emotion in her voice, sincerity and pain as well.

'I hate the system. I hate that Salvington can only be saved by a son, I loathe the laws that say that, and I intend to keep fighting against them as my father has done ever since I was born.' Rob nodded—it was no secret that Lord Salvington was extremely vocal on the need for the laws to change. 'I wish, so wish that I was planning a family just because I want one, that there wasn't this need, that it wouldn't make any difference if the baby is a girl or boy.'

'I know,' he said softly.

She shook her head and he could see a tear glistening on the ends of her eyelashes. 'You don't. You can't.'

Only a little bit he did and somehow it seemed important to tell her that. 'I can in a different way. I don't like the idea of bringing a child into the world with their destiny preordained—that they will have to do their duty, have to be an earl or a countess simply by dint of their existence. Like you I wish I could have a family without any expectations or rules involved.' Since he'd drawn his first breath he'd been brought up to understand the importance of being heir, had duty drummed into him. He wouldn't bring up his child the way he had been brought up, but he couldn't change some facts.

'But if we do it right our child won't see it as a duty they don't want, they will see it as a duty they embrace. I hope they will love their land and their home.'

'So do I, but I wish they could just love it rather than be responsible for it.'

'I understand, but… I don't know about you, but I'd like a large family.' Her tone dreamy. 'A whole brood of kids, and I think that will make a difference. It will take the pressure off the heir and they can share the responsibilities of the estate. If the eldest doesn't want the title, maybe it can be abdicated to the next in line? Maybe it won't be straightforward, but the important thing will be that we are there for them. To talk and listen and help.'

'And love them for them, whether they are a boy or a girl, the eldest or the youngest.'

Her grey eyes were wide and dreamy and an image filled his mind: himself and Adriana sitting in front of a roaring log fire with a mass of kids around them. Two boys, two girls—why not?

She blinked, took a deep breath, pushed her fringe away from her eyes. 'So will you do it? Will you marry me?'

CHAPTER SIX

MARRY. MARRY. MARRY. The word seemed to dance in front of her eyes, hop and twirl elusively out of her reach as she waited for his answer. Would he marry her?

'Are you sure this is what you really want?' he asked.

'Yes.' She wanted to save her land, her home, the home of her ancestors. She wanted her children to play in the woodlands, roam the fields. She wanted to be part of Salvington's future. She had no problem with the lack of love—she was used to that. If she could live with someone who offered her respect and liking it would be a massive improvement on her current status. So it was a no-brainer really.

The only shade of doubt was about whether it was fair to marry him. Could she be the countess he wanted? Step into his mother's no doubt fashionable shoes? Stella could have. Could she? She'd have to.

'Yes,' she repeated. 'It is. It is what I really want.'

'Then this is what I propose.' He leant back in his chair, sipped his wine. 'I am still worried you are rushing into this. So let's give ourselves a few weeks. Time for us to get to know each other better. Make *sure* this is what we both want.'

Relief flooded her and she knew her smile bordered on goofy. 'Fair enough. So what shall we do to get to know each other better? Maybe something we can do just you and me?'

A heartbeat of a pause and the words seemed to hover in the air, swirl and twirl and glitter with an innuendo she hadn't meant at all. Worse, her hand went up to her mouth, brushed her lips, which tingled in memory of the kiss. His lips quirked upwards in amusement and she tried to think of something to say, anything at all. 'You choose.'

He raised his eyebrows. 'You sure?' He stroked his chin. 'Hmm. Something for just you and me. Let me think…an activity of some sort, just you and me…something fun…'

His eyes met hers, then dropped to her lips

and she shivered, would have sworn she could feel the heat of his gaze caress her skin.

Then he grinned at her. 'How about ice skating?' The suggestion was so unexpected she blinked. 'Unless you have something else in mind?'

Her eyes narrowed but she couldn't help grinning back; it felt strange to be teased like this. But it was a short-lived smile once she actually considered his suggestion properly. 'Ice skating sounds fine.' Though actually it didn't—she hadn't been skating since she was a child, when her father's glowering presence had caused her to stumble and fall whilst Stella had glided and twirled. It hardly seemed a milieu where she was going to exhibit the grace and poise a wannabe countess should possess.

But, given she was proposing to marry the man, she could hardly refuse to go ice skating. *Marry. Marry. Marry.* Once again the word swirled in her mind and Adriana wondered if she had lost the plot completely.

'Have you completely lost the plot?' Stella's voice was agitated as she paced the floor of Adriana's bedroom.

'No,' Adriana said quietly. 'I want to do this.

If I have a baby boy it makes us safe. Makes Salvington safe.'

'And what if I then have a legitimate son in the future?'

'Then I am good with that. Your son will be heir.'

'But the sacrifice will be yours. This is my fault.'

'No, it isn't. You couldn't have married Rob and pretended the baby was his. And you couldn't have married Rob if you have feelings for someone else.'

Stella shrugged. 'Yes, I could have. My feelings for this man are irrelevant, pointless, and most of all they are foolish.'

Adriana studied her sister's face. 'If you could turn the clock back, would you change things? Do you wish you'd never met him?'

'Of course I do.' Stella twisted her hands together and gave a half-laugh. 'No, dammit. I wouldn't change a thing. How can I wish this baby away? I can't. As for the father… I don't know, Ria. I never thought I could feel like this. Feel so much.'

'Then…surely you need to tell him about the baby.'

'I'm not going to do anything yet. But this is not about me. You can't marry Rob.'

'You were going to.'

Stella hesitated. 'That's different. I was brought up knowing I would need to marry and have an heir. I chose a marriage of convenience, I wanted to be a countess and it felt fair that I should do it. After everything, after the way Father treats you, you don't deserve to be the sacrifice.'

'It's not about sacrifice. Salvington is ours, our family home, and it is wrong we should lose it. Plain wrong.'

'OK. But why Rob? Isn't there someone else? Someone you like, someone who makes you feel something? A spark?'

Adriana focused on the wave and swirl of her printed duvet, traced the outline of the flowers with her eyes. Imagined painting the actual flower. Hoped her sister couldn't see her face, the tinge of heat as she suddenly recalled the kiss. The way it had sent her body and brain into a whirl and swirl of feeling, desire, need.

'I do like Rob. I think we can make it work. But it's not a done deal. We're going to see how it plays out over the next few weeks.'

Her sister sighed. 'Keep me posted.'

'I will. And what about you?''

'Mum says Father still doesn't want to see

me and it's better he is kept as calm as possible, so I am going to go away for a while.'

Adriana couldn't help but wonder if she was going to find her mystery man. 'Good luck. And you keep me posted too.'

Rob knocked on the front door of Salvington Manor, stepped back as the imposing door swung open to show Adriana. There it was again, a tightening of his chest, an urge to step forward and drop a kiss on her lips. She was dressed simply in dark blue jeans and a chunky-knit jumper that reached mid-thigh, her hair pulled back into a ponytail.

'Morning,' he said.

'Good morning.' She pushed her fringe away and looked up at him briefly. 'I'm ready to go.' She smiled. 'I think, anyway. Though I have the feeling I may be about to make a complete fool of myself.'

'You'll be fine,' he said easily, though he caught a note of what sounded like genuine anxiety in her voice.

'That's easy for you to say. I'm assuming you know how to ice skate,' she said as they walked towards his car.

'Yes, I do, and I'm sure you'll pick it up easily.'

'Hopefully. But last time I tried I spent most of the time flat on my face. I think it's because I was born clumsy.'

'No one is born clumsy and you don't seem clumsy to me.'

She raised her eyebrows. 'I tripped into your arms in the restaurant and yesterday I broke a plate in your kitchen. I rest my case.'

'I think nerves played a part in both those mishaps—you don't need to be nervous now.'

'Hard ice, skates and me; the combination isn't promising.'

'I think it's very promising, and anyway, you're forgetting the magic ingredient.'

'What's that?'

He grinned at her. 'Me.'

Satisfaction touched him as she returned the smile. 'You're magic, are you?'

'Yup. With me you have nothing to fear.'

'I think you're overestimating your talent.'

'And I think you're underestimating yours.' On impulse he took her hands in his, felt her body freeze for an instant, knew the contact had jolted her as much as him. Sensed too that she did always underestimate herself, he just didn't know why. 'This is going to be OK. You can do this—I know you can. We'll take it slow. OK?' He squeezed her hand gently.

'OK.' Her smile was slightly tremulous. 'Sorry. I'm being a complete baby about this.'

'No need to apologise.' That was something he sensed she did far too much of. He squeezed her hand again. 'Let's go.'

He watched as she pressed her lips together as they approached the ice. 'It's fine to hold on to the side for a bit.'

'Why don't I watch you for a turn? Maybe I can learn by osmosis.'

'Nice try. I'll get you started first. So hang on to the edge and find your balance, get comfortable on the ice. Walk round taking small steps.'

'That's it?'

'To start with, yes. If that's OK.'

'That's perfect.' She smiled at him, as if in relief, and he watched her small frown as she focused on finding her feet, her concentration absolute as they circled the rink. 'Right. I think I've got it. What now?'

'Move away from the side a little, bend your knees a bit and relax…again, just feel comfortable. I'll be right here.'

Belatedly it occurred to him that perhaps this was foolish, because the proximity was doing funny things to his head. Her light floral scent cast some sort of spell on him and close up he could see the gloss of her hair, see the slanted angle of her cheekbone, the curve of her lips and…

'Oh, I forgot. I thought this may help on the ice. Hold still.'

He dipped his hand into his pocket and pulled out the small bag, opened it up and showed her what he'd bought. Suddenly wondered if she'd be insulted. 'I thought, just for skating, it may be easier…' He held out the hair clips, dark red barrettes. 'But…'

'That's really thoughtful.' Her smile was wide and genuine as she reached out to take them and stumbled. Swiftly he reached out and caught her, steadied her before she could fall.

'I'll do it,' he said. Oh, so carefully, he unclipped one of the barrettes, desperately aware of her nearness, the feel of her hand on his arm. As he gently brushed her fringe back, the silken glossiness captivated his fingers. He slid the barrette in and now he could see her eyes close up, large, and clear, the grey pulling him in, eyes that could glimmer silver, or cloud to stormy grey, sparkle or cast allure. Any which way they were beautiful, fringed with long brown lashes, and the words fell from his lips without thought. 'Why do you hide such beautiful eyes?'

'I...don't hide them.' Yet she looked away as though she missed the safety of her fringe.

'You are hiding them now,' he countered, and, gently putting a finger under her chin, he tipped her face up. 'You shouldn't.'

'I prefer it,' she said lightly. 'I've always thought people will know what I'm thinking if they see my eyes.'

'And is that a bad thing?'

'It depends what I'm thinking,' she said softly.

And now their gazes meshed together. 'I bet I know what you are thinking now.'

How he wanted to kiss her, and he knew he would have if life hadn't intruded in the form of a teenager who shot past, stumbled and nearly crashed straight into them. Rob moved instinctively to protect Adriana and get them both out of the way and she gave a small, rueful smile.

'Saved,' she said.

'For now,' he answered. 'But we're here to teach you to skate. So let's try to start a glide.' He moved to face her. 'I'll skate backwards, and I'll keep one hand under yours for you to grab if you need to.'

She took a deep breath and nodded, and pushed herself off the side.

'That's it! You're doing brilliantly. See if you can glide for a bit, try and coast. Fabulous.' After a moment he took both her hands in his and skated backwards, drawing her along, saw her lips turn up into a wide smile. The next half-hour flew past and by the end of it he was genuinely impressed. 'See. You're a natural. That's what you were born—a natural skater.'

'You're forgetting the magic ingredient. You. You're a natural born teacher.'

'Then prove it. Have a go on your own.'

At first he thought she'd refuse, and then she nodded. 'OK, but if I fall over...'

'If you fall over that's OK,' he said softly. 'Everyone falls over sometimes. It doesn't mean you're clumsy, or a bad skater. It means you're learning. If you fall over, you get up and off you go. But if you do fall over, fall safely. And I'll be here to help you up. Deal?'

'Deal.' But she didn't fall over. He watched as she pushed away from the side, glided forward, ponytail bobbing up and down as she negotiated around another skater, and a sudden pride slid through him. Because he sensed that this had been harder for Adriana than she was letting on. Seconds later she crashed into the wall next to him. 'Next time perhaps you'd better teach me how to stop. But now the least

I can do is buy you a hot chocolate. To say thank you.'

As they walked back to the car, takeaway hot chocolates in their hands, she said, 'Really, thank you. Once you made me see falling over was OK, it made all the difference. It took the fear away, and you were so patient—you didn't expect me to instantly get it and you didn't get angry when I did something wrong.'

The words caused him to wonder who had taught her in the past, but before he could work out how to ask that she continued.

'But you were pretty impressive—did you learn as a child?'

'No.' His parents would never have let him do anything so 'dangerous' as a child, nothing that could possibly hurt him. And no amount of persuasion could make them see that the chances of his dying on an ice rink…a rugby pitch…climbing a tree…riding a horse…were minuscule. 'I learnt in the States.' Fleur and her boyfriend, Jonathan, had been shocked that he'd never been, had taken him along and he'd loved it, the freedom of gliding across the ice, in control of his movements, able to weave in and out, go backwards…it was something he loved doing. Found too that on the ice ideas seemed to come to him, and he and Fleur had spent hours brainstorming ideas for Easel.

'Tell me about your time there,' she said now and for a moment he wanted to. Wanted to tell her about Easel Enterprises, his pride and joy. But he couldn't. Needed to keep his involvement in Easel Enterprises completely under wraps—it was important to him that this company launched and succeeded as the brainchild of Fleur Hardcastle with an honorary mention to a plain Rob Wilmington, but not a whisper of Viscount Rochester.

For now. Once the company was up and running, once he'd sorted out Darrow, then it would be different, but for now he didn't want the press or his parents or anyone to know, and that meant telling no one.

There was no reason not to trust Adriana but equally no way would he risk trusting her either. After all, he'd trusted Emily with a blind trust that had been repaid with betrayal.

'I enjoyed myself,' he said instead. 'I enjoyed being plain Rob Wilmington, I enrolled on various courses, I travelled, I did normal jobs. I worked in a bar, I worked as a waiter, I went to watch American football.'

'Are you happy to be back?' she asked, and the question took him by surprise.

'Yes.' Realising how terse the answer was, he tried to clarify. Because he had no regrets about coming back. 'I do miss the freedom of my life there, but I do know it was time to come back. My parents are getting older, they want to step back, and I am keen to start work here.'

Her large grey eyes studied him and she nodded. 'I know how hard your parents have worked for Darrow and I think there is a huge potential to build on everything they've done.'

Rob nodded, knew he should feel way more enthusiasm than he in fact did, but it was hard, hard because all his life Darrow had felt like a weight rather than a joy.

'Speaking of your parents, have you told them about me?'

'Yes. I told them that Stella pulled out and that you and I are considering marriage.' He kept his voice neutral but clearly not neutral enough.

'I'm sorry. I'm sure they were disappointed.'

'They…' He hesitated as he recalled the conversation with his parents.

Did you even try to change her mind?' his father had asked.

'No. What would have been the point? I

could hardly marry a woman who loves some-one else.'

His mother had sighed…a small, elegant exhalation of air.

'Darling, I am sure you could have persuaded Stella that what you have to offer far outweighs love. I have no doubt she will soon regret this decision—I do think your father is right. You must at least try.'

'I'm afraid I disagree. I will have no part in forcing a woman to marry me when she doesn't want to. Nor do I wish for a reluctant bride. So I will not be speaking with Stella. However, Adriana and I are considering an alliance. But it is early days.'

'I remember Adriana. She isn't a patch on her sister. Too shy, too gauche.'

Rob had gritted his teeth. *'Well, thank you for your opinion, Mother, but with all due respect it's not up to you who I marry.'*

Her next sigh had been on an industrial scale.

'Given how right we were about Emily, I do think you could listen to us, Rob.'

'You were not right about Emily—you disliked her because of her birth and her status.'

'Very well.' His father's voice had been sharp. *'The important thing is that a mar-*

riage may come from this and Adriana's birth is good. Why don't we meet her? Come, Cecilia, from what I remember Adriana is perfectly presentable. We should give her a chance.'

His mother had nodded.

'Fine. If she wants to speak to me, I'm happy to tell her more about being a countess and what it entails. Why not bring her to dinner on Friday?'

'They would like to meet you,' he offered now, 'but I said it was probably a bit early in the proceedings.' Especially as he suspected his mother's idea may well be to scare Adriana off.

She laid a hand on his arm. 'It's OK, Rob. I'd rather you were honest. I understand why they wanted Stella as a daughter-in-law. I do. She would have found it easy to step into your mother's shoes. In some ways they are very similar—they always know the right clothes to wear, the right things to say. They are at ease in society. Stella was born to be a countess.'

Her voice held no bitterness, was simply factual, but it made him frown.

'Anyone can be a countess,' he stated firmly.

'That is technically correct, but I am pretty sure your parents disagree. But that's OK—it sounds like they are at least willing to give me a chance.' She hesitated. 'And maybe I should meet them sooner rather than later? I mean, who better to tell me about being the Countess of Darrow than your mother? And if they want to meet me and I refuse, that will be bad for any future relationship I might have with them, won't it?'

Her words made sense but a qualm still struck him. One he pushed away—what could go wrong at a simple family dinner? Especially as he would be right there. 'If you're sure,' he said.

She nodded. 'I'm sure.'

CHAPTER SEVEN

ADRIANA LOOKED AT her reflection and wondered what had possessed her to agree to a
family dinner with Rob's parents. Part of it
had been the sheer adrenalin that had coursed
through her after their ice-skating session.
But some of it had logic—she had no doubt
they would prefer Stella as a daughter-in-law
and she completely understood that. But they
couldn't have Stella so it was her job now to
get them on side with her. Get them to accept
that she would at least be a viable substitute.
And she knew the Earl and Countess—had
met them at various events over the years—
and she knew Stella had got on with them fine.

Another look at her reflection—perhaps she
should have bought a new dress, but she'd decided it was better to stick to what she knew
and was comfortable in. A simple grey dress,
bought to allow her to blend into the back-

ground, but she was pretty sure it classed as 'smart casual'.

Now for her hair. She'd keep it loose… Her fingers hovered over the barrettes and her skin tingled as she recalled Rob clipping her hair back, how near they had been to another kiss. Determinedly she clipped her fringe back; a light layer of make-up and she was good to go.

The knock on the door heralded Rob and she ran lightly down the stairs, pulled the door open and gulped. Wondered if he would ever stop having this impact on her. If they did get married would her knees still wobble when they were both old and grey? The thought was enough to stop her in her tracks.

'Hey,' he said softly, and in the dusk she could see that he was smiling down at her, and her heart did a somersault.

'Hey.' With an effort she summoned up some conversation. 'How was your day?'

'Good.' They headed for his car. 'I've been up in London all day. How about you? How was your day?'

'Good too. I spent most of the day in the woodlands overseeing some tree felling. I just hope I don't have woodchips in my hair.'

He glanced across at her quickly before returning his attention to the road. 'So you really are hands-on.'

'Of course. I mean, I do get involved in the books and records side as well.' Thankfully the estate manager employed by her father had a much higher regard for her abilities than her father did. 'Martin, the estate manager, is happy to teach me. Probably because I used to follow him around a lot when I was a child.'

'So he approves of your ideas?'

'Yes. But he does also appreciate my father's position as well.'

'And what about Stella? Is she interested in the land in the same way?'

'No. That's my side of it. I'm focusing on the woodlands right now. Whilst some felling is necessary we need to make sure we are replanting as well. I want Salvington to be environmentally positive and there are so many ways of doing that. I'd like to introduce eco farming and a wildlife area and...' She broke off as she realised they were nearly at Darrow. 'Sorry, I'm rabbiting on. Maybe I am a little nervous about this.'

'No need. I'll be right by your side to make sure my parents are on their best behaviour. And you aren't rabbiting. I'm interested.'

He pulled into the gated sweep of the driveway, but as he drove over the gravel he slowed down. 'What the hell?' His lips set in a grim line. 'Adriana, I'm sorry. We've been ambushed—it looks like my mother has invited more guests than just you tonight. I didn't know.'

Adriana surveyed the row of cars that lined the parking area. 'More guests? But why would she do that?' Stupid question. It was a test—to see if Adriana could cope, to see how she performed in society. 'Don't answer.'

'I won't. But I won't subject you to this either. We're going.'

Adriana thought, and then said, 'No. I will not run away.'

'But you hate parties,' he pointed out. 'And this is outrageous behaviour.'

'Yes, it is. But if we leave, how does that look? To all the guests she has invited—guests who, if we do get married, I will need to socialise with, need to mix with? That's what you want, isn't it? A countess who can step into your mother's shoes? Then I need to start now, because believe me, if I turn tail and run now they will all remember it.'

'So we're going in.'

'We're going in.' Adriana closed her eyes. She could do this; she'd been to parties before, she'd blend in, be as invisible as possible. Get through it, because if she wanted to marry Rob, save Salvington, then she had to.

Before she could change her mind she climbed out of the car and headed for the front door.

'Hey. Hold up. We're going in together, remember?' She halted and he came to her side, took her hand in his, and she took comfort from his proximity, managed a smile for the stately figure of the butler.

'Good evening,' he intoned. 'Come this way.'

They followed him into the drawing room and Adriana quickly scanned the room, her heart sinking as she assimilated the guest list. Members of prominent society families, the older generation here were mostly friends of her parents, people who she'd known since childhood. That wasn't a massive problem, though she suspected those with daughters would prefer Rob to choose his bride elsewhere.

More of an issue was the fact that said daughters were also present, along with others of her contemporaries, young men and women who had always despised her, sensed her vulnerabilities and insecurities in her childhood, and when Stella wasn't around they had delighted in tormenting her.

And in that moment all those childhood feelings resurfaced, but she forced a smile to her face as the Countess approached them, flanked by Lady Eleanor Maxwell, a dazzling redhead who had been one of Adriana's prime tormentors. Both women, the older and the younger, looked immaculate. More than that, they looked svelte, elegant and poised, casting her grey dress into the category of dowdy, boring and plain.

'Hello, Rob, darling. And this must be Adriana. I haven't seen you since you were a gawky teenager. It is marvellous to see you again.'

'You too.' The words sounded stiff and she felt Rob's hand squeeze round her in reassurance.

'You didn't tell me there'd be company,' Rob said.

'Oh, I'm sure I did. But if I didn't I'm sure Adriana doesn't mind. Do you?'

'Of course not.'

'Well, I do,' Rob said. 'So I'm afraid we won't be able to stay long.'

'But it's a three-course dinner, darling. You don't want Adriana to miss out on Marco's cooking, surely.'

Rob's eyes narrowed, and now it was Adriana who squeezed his hand, trying to convey that she really didn't want a scene, especially under Eleanor's amused gaze anyway.

As they followed the Countess further into the room, she could feel herself flinch, wanted to tug the clips out of her fringe and hide as everyone turned to look at her. She heard a repressed snicker from the younger people and knew as she looked at them how wrongly dressed she was.

'Come on, Adriana, say hello to everyone,' Lady Eleanor purred.

'And Rob, your father wants a quick word before dinner,' the Countess interpolated.

As she followed Eleanor towards the small group of younger people Adriana could only hope these people had grown kinder since their childhood days. Wished cravenly that she had Stella to protect her as her sister always had. But now she was on her own, and even as she stepped forward she failed to see a rug, tripped and stumbled.

'Oh, Adriana. Still as clumsy as ever,' drawled Eleanor. 'Now tell us what's going on, darling. We simply don't believe you are dating Rob…'

'In fact, we've all got a bet on how long it will take for Eleanor to cut you out,' said her brother, a dark-haired man who she had always loathed.

It was all so beautifully done—they would claim it was banter, but it didn't feel like it. Stella would know how to handle it, but she didn't. So she tried to smile, and when she had the chance she slipped away to hide in the bathroom. Pulled the clips out of her hair—foolish perhaps but it helped her feel hidden.

The dinner bell rang and she exited the bathroom and followed the other guests towards the dining hall. The massive mahogany dining table was set with the gleam of family silver, place mats adorned with the family crest, an array of cutlery you needed a manual to navigate and designer crystal glasses.

Marvellous. A quick look at the place cards showed that she'd been put next to the Countess and one of her father's oldest friends, Sir Roger Montacue. Whilst Rob was at the other end of the table next to Eleanor.

'How's your poor father?'

'He is stable, thank you.' Adriana smiled politely as a bowl of soup was set down in front of her.

'Glad to hear it.' With that Sir Roger turned

away to engage in a heated conversation about hunting and recent proposed changes to the law.

Then smoothly from her left, 'I thought it would be nice if we had a chat,' the Countess stated. 'I want you to know how dear Rob is to us and to the estate.'

'I am sure he is,' Adriana said quietly as she followed the Countess's gaze to Rob and Eleanor, saw the red-haired woman lean in towards Rob. Distracted, she lifted a spoonful of soup to her mouth, and to her horror a few drips escaped, staining the front of her dress. And of course it was tomato soup. Or roasted tomato and basil bisque, as it was called on the ornately scrolled menu cards.

The Countess continued, her melodious voice light and low, though her eyes were fixed pointedly on the stain, 'We want only what is best for him. Sometimes Rob gets quixotic ideas in his head, favours doing the "right" or "PC" thing without considering the long-term.' She sipped her wine. 'And don't all children always like to do what their parents don't want them to do? But hopefully Rob has learnt his lesson from the past. Now we are so glad to see him back here, where he belongs. And how is your lovely sister? Such a shame she couldn't be here today.'

Well, that told her, and all Adriana could think to say was, 'Yes. It is a shame.'

Because as she looked round the table she could see exactly what the Countess was trying to show her, the reason for this whole dinner, a stunt, a set-up to show Adriana the stark reality, the truth: Rob belonged here. Adriana didn't. Stella did. *Lady* Eleanor did. She saw the red-headed woman's hand touch Rob's arm, heard her soft laughter, wondered if her touch affected Rob, realised it didn't matter. Lady Eleanor was countess material, Adriana wasn't. They'd agreed that attraction was important but not the be-all and end-all.

At that moment she saw him frown, say something to Eleanor that wiped the smile off her face and made her remove her hand from his arm, a faint flush on her cheek. He looked across the table and met her gaze, and as a footman removed his plate Rob whispered something in his ear.

The man nodded, put the plate back down and came round the table to Adriana. 'The Viscount has asked me to let you know that unfortunately he has just got a message that necessitates your departure.'

Before Adriana could respond she saw Rob rise from his place, and now he came to join them. 'Deepest apologies, Mother, I'm afraid I will have to drag Adriana away from this wonderful dinner. A friend of mine called and he needs my help. It's a bit of a crisis so we'll have to run.'

Adriana saw the Countess's lips compress for a fraction of a second and then she rose to her feet and the occasion.

'Oh, darling, I am so sorry. And I hope the crisis is averted; if anyone can help I know you can.' She clapped her hands together and the conversation around the table stopped. 'Unfortunately Rob and Adriana have been called away.'

'Apologies, but we have no choice. Please, all of you continue with dinner and enjoy Marco's wonderful food. And *we'll* no doubt see you at the next event.'

Adriana managed, 'It was lovely to meet you all. And thank you, Cecilia, so much for inviting me.' She gave a small wave and followed Rob out of the room.

As soon as they reached the sanctuary of the car he turned to her. 'I can only apologise. I have no idea what that dreadful gathering was about or what my mother was thinking.' Anger roiled inside him at his mother's temerity in not only not warning them dinner had meant a formal gathering but also separating Adriana from him and making a blatant attempt to throw Eleanor at him. 'But believe me, I will be having words with her.'

'There's no need,' she said. Her voice was oddly colourless.

'There is every need.'

'Do you really have a friend in crisis?' she asked.

'Nope. I wanted to get us out of there pronto.'

'You mean you wanted to rescue me.'

'Rescue *us*,' he corrected as he started the car. 'Now I intend to drive us somewhere nearer to you to have dinner.'

'Actually, I'm not hungry.'

A quick glance at her showed that her hands were twisted together and her face looked pinched with worry, though her fringe once again obscured her eyes.

'What's wrong?'

'You shouldn't have had to rescue me,' she burst out. 'I should have been able to hold my own in there. And I do understand why your mother did it.'

He didn't reply for a while, waited until he

saw a small woodland car park, a local place where people parked to walk their dogs. It was empty now and he pulled in, switched the engine off and turned to face Adriana.

'Then perhaps you could explain it to me.'

Her face was illuminated by moonlight as she nodded. 'Your mother was trying to show me that I don't belong, that I can't step into her shoes. Whereas Lady Eleanor could. I am not countess material. Stella would have waltzed in there and charmed everyone. Eleanor commanded the room. I lack the poise needed, the dress sense, the ability to know what to say. I hid in the bathroom, for Pete's sake.'

Rob shook his head. 'We were ambushed.'

'Yes, we were, but I know I should have coped better and I didn't. I am not sure I can be the countess you want…not sure I can keep my part of the bargain. I want to give you, give both of us the chance to think about that. So if you could drive me home now that would be great. Maybe talk in a couple of days.'

'I…' He could see the misery on her face, knew too that she had loathed the entire time at that dinner. And who could blame her? Every instinct told him to pull her into his arms, kiss away the sadness in her eyes, tell her it would all be all right. But that wouldn't be honourable. If she married him Adriana would be a countess. Dinners like tonight's would abound in her future. That was the way it was. It was imperative that she go into this with her eyes wide open. 'Fine. We'll regroup in a couple of days.'

Adriana opened her eyes to the insistent ring of the phone. Squinted at the window, where dawn was only just emerging. Great. She'd only managed to fall asleep an hour ago, unable to get her dilemma from her mind. Was it fair to marry Rob to get what she wanted when she wasn't sure she could provide him with what he wanted? She didn't know the answer, only knew that the thought of not seeing Rob again felt… wrong.

Irrational hope flared that maybe the caller was him, but of course it wasn't. It was the manager of the riding school they leased the stables to.

She listened and then swung her legs out of bed. 'It's not a problem. I'll be down in fifteen minutes. It's fine.'

And actually it was. In some ways this was exactly what she needed—two stable hands had called in sick and they needed some help. Well, good. The company of horses was exactly what she needed today—better than bloody human beings. An hour later she was immersed in her tasks, wiped a mud-encrusted hand across her face.

'Good morning.'

Adriana whirled round and gave a small gasp, blinked and stared at Rob. 'What are you doing here?'

'I came to talk to you.'

She narrowed her eyes. 'I thought we agreed to wait a couple of days.'

'I thought it was more of a guideline. You said we should go away and think—well, I have, and here I am, ready to share my thoughts.'

'I'm working.'

'I'll help.'

'I don't think it's your sort of thing.'

He raised his eyebrows. 'Based on?'

'Intuition. I mean, have you ever mucked out a stable?'

'As it happens, no. So are you saying I don't belong here?'

Now she narrowed her eyes further. 'Why do I feel I just walked into a trap? Anyway, that's not what I am saying. I am saying you don't know how to muck out a stable.'

'Because I've never done it before. It doesn't

mean I can't learn. If I want to. And I do. So tell me what to do. And I'll help.' He shrugged off his jacket and she couldn't help it; her eyes drank in the fluid movement, the powerful breadth of him.

'You'll get your clothes dirty.' The inanity of the warning struck her.

'I get I'm not dressed right but that's because I wasn't prepared, didn't know I'd be mucking out a stable. Remind you of anything?'

She sighed. 'You cannot compare you being in a stable yard to me being at that dinner yesterday.'

'I think I can. Anyway, I don't mind a little dirt.' He squatted down and scooped up a handful of mud and smeared it on his shirt. 'There, see?'

The laugh was startled out of her. 'Do you even like horses?'

'Time to find out. But if I don't I'll still give it a try. And I'm pretty sure they can't be worse than some of yesterday's guests.'

She watched as he approached the horse she was standing with, saw that his stride was easy, showed no sign of anxiety.

'This is Rusty,' she said. 'He's one of the children's favourites. All these horses are part of a riding school we let the stables to.'

'So what's the best way to approach him?' he asked.

'Are you nervous?'

'A little. He is larger and more powerful than me and I respect that. So I know to be careful but I'm not scared. But I don't want to spook him either.'

'You can stroke his nose. He likes that, don't you, Rusty?' The horse nudged her gently and she smiled at him affectionately, watched as Rob reached out to do the same. 'You can give him a treat. I don't do treats often, because it's not good for them to expect a treat, but I think Rusty is due one. Here.'

She reached into her jacket pocket and pulled out a finger of carrot, which she handed over.

'So what's the best way of doing it? I can see how big his teeth are.'

'Hold the carrot in the palm of your hand and curl your fingers slightly.' She placed her own hand under his, felt an extra frisson to add to the hormonal tumult of his proximity. 'You need to guide your hand upward and don't flinch from the teeth. That's when a horse may start to lunge for the treat.' She knew Rusty wouldn't, he was a prime favourite with the kids and an expert at taking treats from small hands let alone an adult's. She couldn't help studying the shape of Rob's hand anew, marvelled that a hand could evoke such a tug of desire in her. Perhaps it was the sheer capability of it that gave it such beauty. Whatever it was, the contact played havoc with her senses even as she focused on his reaction to Rusty as the horse gently nuzzled from his hand and he smiled.

'You're a good boy, Rusty.' He turned to her. 'Now put me to work,' he said.

'OK. We need to muck out another stall. Basically, use a pitchfork to get together all the manure and soiled straw and then we heap it into the wheelbarrow. But don't pile it up too high. Then we repeat till we've got rid of it all.'

'So is this part of your regular duties?' he asked as he worked.

'No.' She realised that she had stopped work, seemingly entranced by watching the flow of his muscles, the lithe strength of his back, the powerful movement of his shoulders. 'A couple of stable hands called in sick, so I said I'd help out. It's on more of an ad hoc basis. But I do enjoy it. Sometimes I think I prefer the company of horses to people.'

'And if the company behaves like last night's did, who can blame you?' He paused, leant the pitchfork against a wall and turned to her.

'You cannot judge your ability to be Countess of Darrow based on last night.'

She shook her head. 'It's more than that and you know it. Last night showed me how…ill-equipped I am for the position.'

'Rubbish.'

'Excuse me?'

'I said rubbish.'

CHAPTER EIGHT

Rob watched the play of emotions dance across Adriana's features, could see confusion, a hint of ire and a touch of frustration. And the temptation to pull her into his arms, smooth the crease from her forehead, and kiss her nigh on overwhelmed him. She looked ridiculously endearing, with her hair in a messy ponytail, a smear of mud across her nose. Dressed in a wax jacket, leggings and boots, she also looked part of her surroundings, as though she belonged. Which brought him to what he wanted to say.

Now she folded her arms. 'Perhaps you could clarify exactly what you mean by "rubbish"?' She mocked quote marks in the air with vehemence.

'I'm happy to explain. I disagree with your assessment. The bit where you said you couldn't be a countess, couldn't step into my mother's shoes.'

'You saw me yesterday. I let myself be laughed at and bullied, I hid in the bathroom and I even managed to drop soup on myself.'

'That's not what I saw. I saw that you were tricked into a social occasion orchestrated to make you uncomfortable. You didn't turn tail and run, you went in, and in the face of rudeness and provocation you were polite. So what if you spilt some soup? Other people would have poured their soup on my mother's head. Or Eleanor's.'

Now surprise widened her eyes as she studied his expression. 'Thank you. I truly appreciate what you are saying, but part of being a countess is social poise, knowing how to dress, how to talk the talk, host events.'

'Yes, but only part of it. Because I've been thinking and I've realised that when we first discussed our marriage, my expectations, I was wrong. I should never have said you needed to step into anyone's shoes. You can be Countess of Darrow however you want to be. In your own shoes. Or Wellington boots come to that. I wondered if you wanted to be involved with the estate management.'

Now her jaw dropped and he could see a

glimmer of a smile in her eyes along with more than a glimpse of disbelief.

'But I thought that was what you wanted to do.'

'It never occurred to me that it is something you would want to do. And that's my bad.' It was. As he'd driven home the night before, as he'd tossed and turned through a sleepless night, he'd realised how hidebound and pigheaded he'd been and cursed himself for a fool. He'd been so busy ticking boxes, getting the Darrow side of things sorted out so he could get back to also focusing on Easel Enterprises, that he'd done the very thing his parents did to him. He'd not seen Adriana as an individual. 'You can be a countess however you want to be,' he repeated. 'It doesn't have to be done the way my mother did it, or the way Stella or Eleanor would do it. You can do it your way.'

'But... I would love to be involved in the estate but all the other things your mother does are important too.'

'I get that, but I believe you can learn how to do that. Like I am learning how to muck out a stable. I think the only reason *you* think you can't is because you don't believe in yourself.' He just wished he understood why. 'You do have poise. I can see it in the way you move, the way you are here, the way you ice skated. You are more than capable of holding your own—you and I have never had a problem with conversation.'

'That's because you don't scare me. And neither do the horses.'

'Then what does scare you?' he asked softly.

Her eyes held shadows now, that swirled in the grey depths. 'Being judged and found wanting, making a fool of myself, not being good enough.' She blinked as though surprised at the directness of her response.

Again he wondered what made her feel like that, sensed she'd said as much as she wanted to say, or perhaps more as she turned away, headed towards Rusty and stroked the horse's nose.

'Perhaps you judge yourself too harshly,' he said softly. 'And worry too much about what other people think.'

'It's hard not to, though, isn't it?' she asked. 'I do care about being liked. Don't you?'

'To a point,' he said. 'I care about being respected by other people, providing they are people I respect myself. And liked as well, I suppose, and it's important to me to be liked for myself, not for my title.'

She sighed. 'You're the sort of person people do respect,' she said on a sigh. 'I'm not.'

'If you are talking about people like Eleanor and that crowd, I wouldn't give them a second thought. Why would you want them to like you?'

'Because it would have made my life a whole lot easier as a child, and last night for that matter. But you're right. I don't want them to like me, I want them to respect me.' She turned away from the horse. 'I'm guessing you've never had a lack-of-respect issue.'

Part of him wanted to let that assumption lie, didn't want to remember times past, but he wanted to help in some way, wanted to show Adriana that she should believe in herself, that she deserved respect from everyone.

'Actually my childhood held its share of bullies. My parents were so relieved, so happy to have a son. They tried for years and years, went through countless IVF attempts and who knows what else? My mother went to every type of doctor of every type of medicine and eventually when they had given up all hope I came along. A miracle baby. An heir. And they were terrified they'd lose me—that an illness or an accident would carry me off.'

'That's understandable,' she said.

'I know, but they took it to extremes. They wouldn't let me ride a bike, climb a tree, have a scooter. They vetted anyone who went anywhere near me. But my father insisted on sending me to boarding school.' Like all the Earls who had gone before him. 'But under strict instructions not to let me do anything dangerous including sport or pretty much anything extracurricular that held even the possibility of me stubbing a toe. As you can imagine, that put a bit of a downer on my school life. I was teased and bullied.' Mercilessly. He could still recall the taunts, the tricks, the names. The time they'd held him still and poured buckets of water over him, or held him down in a freezing shower to 'teach him to swim'. The pink ribbons they'd put in his hair because he was 'girlie'.

'But didn't you talk to your parents? Explain?'

'I tried, but their take on it was that I needed to "man up" because everything they were doing was for the estate, to ensure the future of the line. To make sure I grew up "to be an earl that history and future generations would be proud of".' He could hear bitterness in his voice and hastened to add, 'But the reason I'm telling you is I do know what it feels like to be bullied and have no respect whatsoever.'

'What did you do?'

'I worked out. I saved my money and I sent off for weights and training stuff. I found a shed on the edge of the school grounds and I set up a makeshift gym. In the holidays I managed to persuade one of the staff to cover for me whilst I went running and I followed a regime. And it worked. My parents were suspicious but so pleased I was apparently bulking up naturally they didn't investigate too hard. When I was ready it was a simple exercise— I challenged the head bully to a one-on-one fight.'

'But surely he saw that you were a real threat.'

'I don't think he did. To him I was still a weakling.' A snivelling cry baby, because once, just once, a single tear had escaped him.

'What happened?'

'I won.' He could still hear the satisfaction in his voice. 'It wasn't the most scientific fight in the world, but the end result was a win for me.'

'And after that?'

'He stopped picking on me or anyone else. And after that I got people's respect.' Especially as in the inevitable aftermath he hadn't 'snitched', though he'd made it clear he would if the bully or any of his mates laid a finger on anyone again.

'I'm glad. Not glad about what happened to you because it makes me angry, but glad that good won out in the end. You saved yourself and others.' Now she grinned at him. 'So what would you suggest? That I challenge Eleanor to a brawl, or perhaps your mother?'

He grinned back. 'I was thinking more subtle than that. Prove them wrong. Show them your way is the right way. Outdress them, outsmart them, make them sit up and take notice. Or show them you don't give a damn. But whatever you do, don't roll over and give up. If you don't want to be Countess of Darrow that's fine, but if you do then do it your way. Don't give up on this, on us, because of those people. Or because you don't believe in yourself.' He stopped. 'So what do you think?'

'I think... Thank you. For believing I can do this. And I'd like to give it a try.'

As she stepped towards him, looked up at him, the air seemed to shimmer, charged by a sense of momentousness. And it seemed inevitable that as she took another step forward he too moved and then the gap was closed and then he was kissing her and she was kissing him. Mutual desire, mutual relief, the same need for each other, and it felt *right* as she melted into his embrace. His whole body hummed with desire for her, for Adriana, as her lips parted under his and he revelled in her taste, her touch, the brand of her hands through the cotton of his shirt. The smell of the stable yard, the rawness of their desire, the vanilla scent and gloss of her hair heightening his every sense.

The sound of someone clearing their throat broke into the moment, slowly penetrated the fog of desire, the bubble of need where only he and Adriana existed, and they moved apart and he saw the interested face of a young woman.

'Clara,' Adriana said in a credible attempt at assurance. 'This is the manager,' she said to Rob by way of explanation.

'Nice to meet you,' he said.

'The stalls are mucked out, and the saddles are pretty much cleaned,' Adriana continued brightly.

'Thank you, Adriana. I really appreciate you coming down to give us a hand.'

Clara was clearly speaking on automatic; her attention was solely on Rob, her eyes slightly narrowed as if she was trying to work it out.

'Right. I need to get back to the house,'

Adriana said briskly. 'Let me know if you need me tomorrow or this evening.'

'Of course. Thanks again.'

Clara turned and left with one more backwards glance, and Adriana shook her head. 'That was a bit embarrassing.' Yet she didn't look embarrassed, her cheeks still flushed and a smile still tipping her lips. 'So what now?'

And just like that Rob knew exactly what they should do next—as each moment went on he became more and more sure that he and Adriana could make a go of a marriage. A wife who actually loved the estate would be a massive bonus—would allow him more leeway to balance Darrow with Easel quicker. 'I have an idea. We've got to know each other better now so let's take it to the next stage. See how we survive spending proper time together.'

'Define proper time,' she said, a hint of wariness in her eyes.

'A week? Spent together away from here, away from our normal lives, away from family, where we can see what it would be like to actually live in the same place. Obviously the beauty of a marriage of convenience is that we can shape it however we like, spend as much or as little time with each other as we want. But we will still be living together and that means spending some time together. We'll get back from work and then what will we do every night?' He paused and gave a sudden smile. 'Don't answer that.'

Heat touched her cheeks. 'I wasn't intending to.' She grinned. 'But if I had been I would have suggested play Monopoly, of course.'

Now he chuckled. 'Of course. But in all seriousness this will give us a chance to see if we are comfortable together, can spend time together without getting on each other's nerves.'

'You mean you want to see if I have any annoying habits?'

'Absolutely. And of course make sure you can put up with mine.'

'So where would we go?'

'How about Portugal? For a week. My parents have a villa there.'

A heartbeat of hesitation and then she nodded. 'Let's do it.'

Adriana looked at her mother. 'So Father still doesn't want to see Stella. Or me.'

Her mother shook her head. 'I'm sorry, Ria. He says he can't. I think…' She hesitated. 'The attack has changed him; I don't know if it will last or not, but he is gentler, kinder, more like the man I used to know. But he's also emotional and depressed—he says he needs to get his head together before he sees anyone. Needs to be more himself—the doctors say it's normal to have a lot of emotional change after an attack. But it's important for him to be positive and rest and look after himself.'

Adriana looked at her mother. 'Will you tell him what I've done, what I'm doing?'

'Yes, I will. When the time is right, but Ria...'

'Yes.'

'Are you sure you want to do this?'

'Of course I am, Mother. I want to make Salvington safe; you know how important that is. It is our home, our place, it belongs to *us*.'

'I know, Ria, and I know how much you love it.'

'So do you, don't you?'

There was a silence. 'I understand how you feel about it, but... Salvington is a place—you are a human being with one life. If, God forbid, your father had died Salvington would have gone to Bobby Galloway, and you would have had to get on with your lives. Salvington is just bricks and stone and mortar and land. It's not more important than your happiness.'

There had been a hint of bitterness in her voice and Adriana got it. 'Oh, Mum. I'm sorry.

Salvington has always been put above your happiness.'

'You're right. Everything in my life has revolved around Salvington since I married your father. I don't want it to ruin your life. If you go ahead with this you give up the chance of love, of a fairy-tale ending.'

Adriana went to her mother and hugged her. 'I don't believe in fairy tales and this won't ruin my life. Truly it won't. I love Salvington. To me it is more than bricks and mortar and soil, it feels like part of me, I feel connected to it and I want it to be part of my life, my children's lives. I *have* to do this.'

'Well, you've always known your own mind, sweetheart. All I can do is wish you luck.'

'Thank you.' Another hug and though her mother smiled Adriana could see the sadness in the smile and the tiniest flicker of doubt pervaded her mind. A flicker she quenched instantly. This was the right thing to do. She knew it. She and Rob had a plan.

CHAPTER NINE

Rob glanced sideways at Adriana, silhou-
etted against the plane window, a background
of blue sky and cloud. She had a book in her
hand and was absorbed in it, and as he studied her he realised how much he liked what he
saw. There was something tranquil about her,
her fringe was clipped back with the barrettes
he'd given her, and she seemed more at ease.
All positives that augured well for their plan—
a sense of the surreal ran through him—he
was possibly—no, probably—looking at the
woman he would marry, have children with,
a family.

Someone who shared his own values and beliefs, who didn't want love and was happy to
broker a partnership. And then there was the
spark between them; the kisses they'd shared
imprinted on his mind and body.

Whoa. Careful here, Rob. Attraction was

what had triggered the whole disastrous relationship with Emily. She'd reeled him in like an expert, teasing, tempting and sweetening it all with a shyness and a pretence that she was falling in love. But attraction had blinded him to the falsity of her words, her actions, her gestures. He'd been played, sure, but he'd let it happen because he'd desired her, because he'd let himself fall in love with her, or with who she pretended to be.

With Adriana there was no risk of love, he'd made that clear from the outset, but he didn't want his judgement clouded by desire. They needed to decide whether they could make a life together, raise a family and live in mutual respect and liking. That was where his focus needed to be.

His email pinged and he looked down to see an update from Fleur: plans for a company launch, how she and Jonathan wished he could be there, how excited they were and ending with a request to call him.

Quickly he typed a reply, promising to call when he could the next day, and for a moment he wished this flight was going to the States, that he was taking Adriana to a dazzling launch, could introduce her to Fleur and

Jonathan, tell her about the company, show her the designs, the concept…

'You OK?'

Instinctively he lowered the laptop screen and turned to look at Adriana, who narrowed her eyes. 'I'm not trying to read your emails,' she said, and ice encased her voice. 'You just seem a bit transfixed, and the pilot has announced we're arriving soon and to put our seat belts back on.'

'Oh.' He clicked his seat belt in and his laptop shut, told himself he couldn't tell her about Easel. It was strictly need-to-know and Adriana didn't need to know. Not yet. Because he could not be one hundred per cent sure he could trust her. He didn't think she'd go public, but how could he be certain? He would never have believed Emily could betray him so thoroughly. In fairness his assessment of Adriana was way more balanced, but even so… if it would benefit Salvington in some way maybe she could be persuaded to break his confidence. An unlikely scenario, but why take the risk?

But he had been rude. 'I apologise,' he said.

She shook her head. 'Sorry you closed the laptop or sorry you weren't more subtle?' she asked, and he couldn't help but smile.

'Touché.' He paused. 'The latter, but I am sorry.'

'Then apology accepted. I understand.'

But he could hear the hurt in her voice as well, a hurt he understood, but could do nothing about. So it was a relief when the plane began its descent and she turned to look out of the window.

Once they'd got their luggage, they picked up the car he'd hired and soon they were headed towards the villa. 'This is utterly beautiful,' she stated. 'What an incredible place to come to for family holidays.'

'It is beautiful,' he agreed. 'We could drive via the road tunnels, which are an incredible constructive feat in themselves. I believe there are over one hundred tunnels and goodness knows how many bridges. But today I thought we could go the scenic route if you don't mind, although it will take a little longer.'

'I'd like that. Thank you.'

Minutes later she gasped. 'The road is so steep it feels impossible that the car can move forward. But the views are utterly breathtaking.'

'I thought we could stop at the top. It's called Cabo Girão and it's the second highest sea cliff in the world. I believe it's about five hundred and eighty metres above sea level.'

She fell silent after that, clearly allowing him to focus on driving until he pulled into the massive car park at the summit.

He turned to face her. 'About ten years ago they built a glass walkway at the lookout point, a suspended platform of transparent glass. Apparently it is utterly incredible, though it can be a little bit scary. I should have checked if you suffer from vertigo.'

'Nope, not a bit. Let's go!'

As they approached the walkway they fell silent. It was late in the day so the tourists were sparse, and Adriana stepped forward and stopped.

'Whoa.'

'You OK?'

'I'm a tiny bit dizzy, but it's one hundred per cent worth it.'

Instinctively he placed an arm round her shoulder to steady her, and perhaps to steady himself as well. The platform jutted out over the sheer drop that plunged down to the swirl of the ocean below.

'It's like walking on air,' she breathed and now she wrapped her arm round his waist as well, the sensation giving him a funny sense of warmth as they stepped forward together. They stood at the railing and stared out over the panoramic vista, the jut and angle of the landscape, the cliff fronts and sweep of mountains, the stretch of rooftops and then down at the churning surf.

'Look. You can see the fields down there,' he pointed out. 'It's odd to see them so near the sea, but they are dried-up lava streams which makes the soil extra-fertile.'

'They are called *fajas*, aren't they?' She smiled up at him. 'I looked up interesting facts about Madeira. But nothing prepared me for this. It is truly spectacular.'

He nodded, knew that the experience was made better in some way by sharing it with Adriana, seeing the genuine appreciation and awe on her face, the feel of her arm round his waist.

'Thank you for bringing me,' she said. 'It must have been amazing coming here as a child and getting to see all these wonderful things.'

'We didn't really do much sightseeing when we were here,' he said. 'And if we had my parents wouldn't have let me anywhere near a cliff edge. I mean, this wasn't built but they didn't even like driving on any road other than the motorways. They thought it was too danger-ous. Some of the roads are pretty narrow and near the edge of very vertiginous cliffs.'

She looked thoughtful. 'Do you think you'll feel like that with your children?'

'No. Or at least if I do I won't act on it. It didn't help me being wrapped in cotton wool. I understand why they did it but at the time I hated it.'

'Of course you did,' she said softly. 'I imag-ine you must have wanted to take all sorts of risks, and after what happened to you at school it must have been even worse that holidays felt restricted too.'

'Yes. It was hard.' And it had been lonely as well: his parents had wanted him to get to know the 'right sort of people' but it had made making friends with any people impossible because of the swathe of restrictions on his activities.

'Speaking of your parents, your mother called me yesterday. To apologise. Was that your idea?'

Surprise touched him. 'Actually, no, it wasn't. I mean, I did make it clear that I thought her behaviour was abominable and we would not be returning to visit them any time soon, but I didn't ask her to contact you. She did that off her own bat. Was it a real apology?'

Adriana grinned. 'Well, to begin with she said she was sorry for "springing" extra guests on me yesterday—that she should have realised it might be a "bit much".'

He sighed. 'So more of a non-apology.'

'Maybe. So I said she didn't need to apologise, that I was *flattered* that she wanted me to meet old family friends.'

Rob emitted a crack of laughter. 'Good for you. What did she say to that?'

'Actually, she laughed too and said, and I quote, "Admirably said, my dear. I deserved that." Then she apologised again and said she hoped we have a good time in Portugal. So I am going to take that as an olive branch.'

'You should. And see?'

'See what?'

'You handled my mother brilliantly. That was the exact right thing to say to her. Which shows you *do* know the right thing to say.'

Her arrested expression made him laugh and he squeezed her a little closer to him.

'What about your parents?' he asked. 'Have you told them?'

He felt her tense slightly and then she spoke, the words careful. 'I told my mother, but she is going to wait to tell my father. When we have made a final decision.' Before he could respond she stepped away from him and turned. 'I guess we'd better get going. Before it gets dark.'

'Sure. Let's go.'

Adriana was aware of Rob's sideways scrutiny as they walked back to the car and she kept up a bright flow of conversation, having no wish to discuss her conversation with her mother, because she still hadn't really had a chance to process it. Perhaps because she didn't want to.

And once they were in the car she fell to silence so he could focus on driving and she could focus on the scenery, the dusk lit by streetlights that illuminated a village full of thatched cottages, flashes of green fields and everywhere the steep cliffs and curves and bends. Until he said, 'Nearly there,' as they wound their way up another vertiginous mountain road.

And then there it was, a glorious villa that looked as though it was nestled into the cliff itself. Dazzling white walls, blue shutters and a terracotta roof all seemed to gleam in the last few shards of sunlight. 'It's beautiful,' she said.

He parked outside and they climbed out of

the car, and she inhaled the smell of the sea, the tang of salt mixed with the scent of hazy sunshine and hibiscus that bloomed in the dusk.

'Come and see inside,' he said, and she followed him in. The villa was open-plan, the large kitchen area well-equipped, the dark marble countertops polished, and leading to a living space complete with wicker armchairs and sofas and luscious green potted plants.

But what caught her attention most was the view, the jut and crag of the mountains, the undulating dark blue of the waves topped with gleams of silver that stretched to meet the horizon, the terracotta roofs of the village houses. As she looked her fingers itched to draw, to try and capture the colours and vibrancy.

'This is amazing—no wonder your parents want to retire here.'

'If you like we could have an evening stroll through the village, find somewhere to eat.'

'That sounds like a plan.'

Ten minutes later they were walking through the picturesque village, and it seemed the most natural thing in the world when he took her hand in his. The village was tiny, only a few hundred metres from end to end, filled with cobbled streets and narrow alleys lined with pretty stone houses and gardens that scented the air with bougainvillea. The whole was interspersed with allotments that boasted grapevines and vegetables galore, and in the middle was a village square with shops and restaurants and a small, white-walled church.

'It's like stepping into a fairy tale,' she said and then almost wished she hadn't. Because the words were a reminder that this wasn't a fairy tale that ended in love and romance and a happy-ever-after.

As if he guessed her thoughts he looked down at her. 'Well, I am very happy to see that this fairy-tale setting has an actual restaurant, so we don't have to rely on finding a gingerbread house.' He gestured towards a small, busy eatery. 'Does this look OK?'

The restaurant overlooked the sea, its glass-fronted exterior showing a scattering of square tables and booths mostly full with customers, families that crossed several generations, young couples and a few people on their own. The door opened and a tantalising aroma of garlic, seafood and spices wafted out. 'Definitely.'

Once inside they both studied the menu.

'What are you going to have?' he asked.

'I'm not sure. What have you chosen?'

'Trying to avoid food envy again?' he asked, and she shrugged, knew it was foolish. 'I've got an idea. Choose whatever you like and I'll do the same and then we'll go halves.'

The sheer thoughtfulness warmed her and she smiled as the waiter approached. 'Thank you. In that case I'll be adventurous and try the *filete de espada com banana frita e maracujá.* The description written in both Portuguese and English sounded amazing. The swordfish fillet would be soaked in a mixture of flour, egg and parsley and slowly fried, then lemon would be added, and it was accompanied by fried banana and passion fruit.

'And I'll have the *arroz de polvo.*' Adriana quickly scanned his choice before handing the menu back and nodded approval. Octopus, rice and a rich base of tomatoes, onions and the chef's very own spice mix.

'Excelente,' the waiter said.

Once the waiter had gone Adriana glanced round the restaurant, this time paying more attention to the people. Smiled as a woman she assumed to be a grandmother reached out and tickled a toddler safely ensconced in a high chair; the whole family laughed as the child giggled with glee and his parents linked hands behind the chair. Next to that table sat a young man and woman, and as she looked the man reached out for the woman's hand and they exchanged a smile so full of love that Adriana felt a sudden unexpected tear prickle her eyelashes.

'Adriana? You OK?' Rob asked.

'Of course. Just people-gazing. I wonder what we look like to them. A couple? Two friends? Work colleagues?'

'I'm not sure.' He frowned. 'Is something wrong?' He turned slightly, studied the tables she'd been looking at. 'If you're having any doubts, tell me.'

'I'm not.' And she wasn't. She knew it didn't matter, knew that once her parents had been like that young couple and after Stella's birth had even been like the other one. It hadn't lasted and yet for a minute she'd wanted to experience what it felt like to be looked at like that.

'Are you sure? You mentioned fairy tales earlier. Are you sure that isn't what you want?'

She smiled sadly at his perceptiveness. 'I am sure.' She waited as their food arrived, thanked the waiter and then looked down at her plate, carefully halved her portion as he did the same. Looked up and met his gaze, saw the slight crease in his brow and knew he didn't fully believe her. 'It just reminded me of something my mother said—that Salvington was only bricks and mortar and wasn't worth giving up the fairy tale for. I guess her saying that surprised me.' She tasted the food and gave a small appreciative nod at the tang of salt and lemon, that complemented the sweetness of the banana and the sour hint of the passionfruit.'

'Because her fairy tale crumbled around her?'

'Exactly. I also hadn't realised that she feels differently about Salvington from the way Stella and I do. I suppose it's natural.' In truth she felt stupid that it hadn't occurred to her before. 'My father's concerns about Salvington destroyed her marriage.'

'It won't be like that for us,' he said. 'I believe there are different types of happy endings. I want us to be happy but our happy-ever-after won't be based on love with its roller coaster of emotions. It may not be a fairy-tale happy ending but I think it has a chance of being a real one. After all, do you really believe Prince Charming and Cinderella had a great marriage based on one party?'

Adriana grinned suddenly. 'That she went to in a pumpkin.'

'And Sleeping Beauty didn't even get the party.'

'Just one kiss.'

The kisses they had shared shimmered across her mind and she knew the same thought crossed his mind as his gaze snagged on her lips.

'I think we're doing this the right way,' he said softly. 'And it's OK for us to get to our happy ending our way. I think our foundations will be stronger than Cinderella's.'

She nodded. 'You're right.' Of course he was and it was time to put her doubts behind her. Her mother couldn't be right—why would Adriana want a happy-ever-after that was based on something as transitory as love? Answer was, she didn't. So, 'Now hand over your plate,' she said as she picked up her own, ready to swap. 'The swordfish was incredible and now I'd like to try the octopus.'

In fact the whole sharing was symbolic of their partnership, a mutual negotiation and agreement that benefited them both. Their relationship wouldn't be based on deceit and illusion like her relationship with Steve had been. Nor on love like her parents' had been. Nor on the vagaries of an attraction that might not last. This was the right way forward.

CHAPTER TEN

ADRIANA OPENED HER eyes, looked up at the bright white of the ceiling, turned her head to see the closed slatted blinds that had plunged the room into darkness and realised she had no idea of the time. Glanced at the luminous dial of her watch and swung her legs out of bed. Eight-thirty, definitely time to get up, follow the tantalising smell of coffee and freshly baked rolls. She showered and pulled on a long grey sundress, pulled her hair back into a ponytail and ventured into the cool, spacious kitchen.

'Good morning. I went down to the bakery and got breakfast,' Rob said.

'That looks divine.' Mind you, she thought, so did he. Hair shower-damp, jeans and a T-shirt that showed the sculpt and breadth of his shoulders, the muscular strength of his legs.

Enough. Focus on the food, on buttering bread, dolloping on jam.

'So what would you like to do today?' he asked.

'Honestly? I'd like to have a lazy morning on the beach, take my book, soak up the sun, then go and do something more energetic in the afternoon.'

'Sounds good to me.' He rose from the table, refilled the cafetiere, his back slightly turned. 'I do have to make a few calls first, some un-expected business—if that's OK. I'll only be an hour or so, if you want to go without me.'

'That's fine.' Though she had the impression he was over-casual, hiding something, want-ing to be rid of her, but dismissed the idea as sheer paranoia. Realised too that this would give her an opportunity to spend an hour alone, a chance to get some sketching done on the beach. She'd brought simple pencils and a sketchbook on the off-chance.

He nodded. 'I'll give you a call before I head down.'

'Sounds good.'

An hour and a half later Adriana was set up on the beach, felt the familiar sense of absorp-tion take over, her whole being focused on try-ing to get her concept of the landscape onto the paper in front of her. To somehow convey the sense of nature's majesty, the unique beauty of the colours and hues and how they made her feel.

So absorbed in fact that she completely lost track of time until she heard Rob's voice.

'Here you are.'

Panic touched her and without even thinking she rose and spun round, every instinct telling her to hide her work.

'Sorry I was so long.' He looked slightly puzzled. 'So what have you been doing?'

'Nothing.' Spinning back round, she picked up her folder, moved to stuff the sketches into it.

'Adriana? What's wrong?' He stepped backwards. 'If you don't want me to see, that's fine. I'll move away. Sort it out slowly.'

She didn't need telling twice. Quickly she put the pencils back, carefully put the sketches back into the folder, cleared the easel away and turned back round. 'You said you'd call,' she said, aware of how petulant she sounded.

'I thought you might be absorbed in your book or napping. I didn't realise you needed to be warned.' He sounded puzzled rather than angry. 'I am guessing you were sketching.'

'It's a hobby. Something I do for myself, so I don't really talk about it.'

'So not something you feel comfortable sharing.'

'Exactly. As I said, I don't want to talk about it.' Forget petulant—now she was being downright rude. 'I'm sorry,' she said.

'Sorry you were rude or sorry you didn't hear me in time?' he asked.

'Touché,' she responded, echoing their conversation on the plane. Only with the roles reversed. In this case she was the one hiding something. 'And the latter. No one knows about it, that's all. Now you do. So…it would be great if you don't mention it. In the unlikely event it ever came up. With my family. With anyone.'

'Fine.' To her surprise he didn't sound at all judgemental. 'If this is something you want kept private, then of course I will make sure it is.' Calmly he placed the rucksack he was carrying on the sand, opened it and took out a blanket. Shook it out and sat down. 'I hope one day when you're ready you'll feel comfortable showing me your work, but I won't pressure you. We're here to get to know each other better but not to intrude on each other's privacy.'

The words should have been reassuring and

yet they made her wonder what he was keeping private from her. What hadn't he wanted her to see on his laptop? She could hardly ask, not when she was unwilling to share her own secret, not when she would have hidden her art from him if she could. And what if his secret was a dark one? After all, she'd trusted Steve, believed in him, and his secret had broken her heart and taken her to the depths of humiliation. She shook the fear off. It had been different with Steve—he'd used her, lied to her, conned her. Rob wasn't doing that—they were negotiating a partnership and within that they were agreeing that each of them had the right to privacy.

She'd just have to trust his secret was as innocent as her own.

'Agreed,' she said and lowered herself onto the blanket, hugged her knees and looked out at the azure blue of the waves.

'Any other hobbies you want to tell me about?' he asked, and now there was a smile in his voice and she told herself to relax.

'Not really. You know I like horses, and I enjoy reading, but most of my spare time I paint.' She pressed her lips together.

'If I promise not to ask to see your work,

would you mind telling me a little bit about it? Like when you started?'

She supposed there was no harm in that. 'I started when I was about twelve—Stella thought she'd like to take up art but then she lost interest. I came across all the stuff one day and thought I'd have a go and I was hooked.' It had provided a safe haven, a way of escaping, of losing herself in another world.

'Were you tempted to take it further, study art at college?'

'No.' The idea of showing her work made her feel too vulnerable, the idea of losing something that gave her so much joy too scary. 'I draw and paint for myself.'

'And that's enough?' He lay back on the blanket, looking up at the sky, and she sensed it was so that she wouldn't feel pressured to reply, and that knowledge did seem to make it easier to speak.

'I love the challenge of getting how I feel onto paper. Capturing a moment and what that is all about. I mean, this landscape here—I don't think it's ever really the same from day to day, maybe superficially it is, maybe one summer's day is very like another, but it isn't really. And not just because the cloud formation is different or the sun slightly less bright. It's also about how a person is seeing the world. If I'm happy, a stormy landscape may look different than it does if I'm sad. I find it interesting how much feelings filter through into our pictures. But it's more than that. It's trying to convey beauty without it being wooden. I mean, it's frustrating sometimes because I don't always know how to achieve a perspective I want, but mostly I love it.' She broke off. So much for not talking, once she'd started it seemed she couldn't stop. 'Sorry. I spouted on for ever.'

'No need to apologise. There is nothing wrong with feeling passionate about something. But…are you sure you don't want to do something with all that passion? Exhibitions and—?'

'No.' The idea was terrifying in the extreme. 'It's something I do for myself. The way other people might go running or cook a lovely meal or go to the gym.'

He frowned. 'I have to admit I am now very curious to see what you were sketching.'

For a second she considered the idea. After all, it wasn't as though he would be rude or put her work down the way her father would. At least he'd be polite. But wouldn't that be just as bad? At the moment she could look at her work and it was hers. She could tell herself that it wasn't too shabby, that it didn't matter if it was. But subjecting it to anyone else's gaze was too risky…think how embarrassed Rob would be if he had to try and find something nice to say whilst inwardly laughing. Or worse still, pitying her delusions.

'Sorry,' she said firmly, shaking her head. 'I…can't.' And she needed to close this conversation down, should never have opened up as much as she had. 'How about we build a sandcastle?' she suggested.

He sat up and turned to look at her, a slightly odd look on his face. 'A sandcastle?'

'Yup. I think it would be fun. I haven't built a sandcastle for years. If you need a better reason, it'll test our ability to work together as a team.'

'I don't need an excuse,' he said. 'I was just remembering the last time I built a sandcastle here. I'd made friends with a local boy. He was called Juan, and he spoke Portuguese and I spoke English, but we managed to communicate well enough to start building a castle. But we only got halfway through before we were stopped.'

'Why?'

'My parents didn't approve of me mingling with the locals. Ridiculous, I know, but they marched me off and that was that. When was the last time you built a sandcastle?'

'Funnily enough, mine never got completed either. My mother took Stella and me on a holiday.' One of her mother's few acts of rebellion. Her father had been in the midst of his affair and her mother had said, 'Right. We're going on holiday.'

It had been wonderful. Relaxed and full of laughter, and the three of them had been engrossed in building a sandcastle when her father had arrived. 'He took over, decided it would be better to turn the whole thing into a contest. Him and Stella versus my mother and me. He and Stella raced ahead and finished and I never got to finish mine.' Hadn't wanted to, all the fun sucked away. 'I've always regretted that lost castle.'

'And I've always regretted mine. So I suggest you and I build the best castle ever. Better than anyone's. Deal?'

'Deal. The key, *I* think, is to have wet sand.'

He nodded. 'Agreed. So I suggest we dig a well so we don't have to keep going and getting water from the sea.'

'Sounds good. But we need spades.'

'I'm pretty sure there were some back at the

villa. Probably the same ones I used all those years ago.'

A quick trip back and he returned, holding out two spades. 'Red or blue?'

'I'll take blue,' she said, and looked down at the choice for an inordinately long time, suddenly way too aware of him, the sculpt of shoulder muscle, the lithe shape of his forearms and those hands that she still craved to feel on her. As she looked up their gazes met and the flash of desire in his blue eyes sent a shiver through her entire body, wobbled her legs and clenched her tummy with an answering tug of need.

Focus.

'Right. Let's start digging.' Her voice was a husk of its usual self as she forced herself to turn away and set to work.

He nodded and squatted down beside her and she gulped at his sheer proximity, focused on the movement of the spade, the trickle of sand, the quest to dig deep enough for water. But somehow the actions, the rhythm, the scent of the sea, the beating of the sun on the back of her neck all combined to heighten her senses, her awareness of him.

He paused to reach for a water bottle, took off the lid and handed it to her, and now she felt the heat of his gaze as she tipped her head back to drink.

To her fevered imagination it seemed that as they built up the layers of the castle, the tension built up alongside it, her awareness of Rob growing alongside the upward spiral of the smooth sand walls, the turrets shaped so carefully—how could his hands be so deft and sure, pay such attention to detail? As she watched the movement of his fingers, the dextrous flick of his wrist, her mouth dried.

And it wasn't only her—she knew it, even if she didn't quite believe it. She caught the lingering of his gaze on her, could feel the tension in his body as they worked together, and most of all she could see it in his eyes, the dark pupils sending goosepimples over her, and when their hands accidentally touched she thought she might actually combust.

Instead she placed the final seashell in place and jumped to her feet. 'Ta-da!'

'Ta-da, indeed.'

'It's…'

'A work of art,' he said, his deep voice full of meaning as he looked not at the castle but at Adriana, and each word shivered over her skin.

'It is,' she agreed. 'I'll…take a picture.' Send it to her mother and Stella. To give herself something to do so she didn't simply throw herself at him. 'It is a masterpiece and it feels very satisfying to have completed it.' She was babbling now.

'Hmm…' he said. 'I'm not sure satisfied is the exact word to describe how I'm feeling.' Her startled gaze went to his and to her annoyance she could feel a blush rising on her cheeks. 'When I said let's go away together I hadn't factored in how…awkward it might be, fighting the attraction factor.' He paused. 'Assuming I'm not the only one feeling it.'

She shook her head. 'Nope. You are definitely not alone.' She gulped.

'Remind me why we're fighting it?'

'Because we both agreed that the attraction box is ticked and to explore it further is unnecessary and may cloud our judgement when it comes to assessing whether or not this marriage is truly a good idea and whether we are compatible in other ways. More important ways.' The words came out in a rush and felt completely meaningless, syllables that were whirled away by the sea breeze. Because right now nothing felt more important than the simmer of desire. She looked at him across the tartan blanket, against the backdrop of sun, sea and sand, and suddenly judgement seemed ir-relevant. She tried to think. 'Or…'

'Yes?' He spoke like a parched man who had seen the glimmer of an oasis.

'Or maybe we're looking at it the wrong way. Right now attraction is still clouding our judgement because all I can think about is the attraction. So maybe acting on the attraction will help. And if it doesn't, well, it doesn't mat-ter.'

'Damned if we do and damned if we don't?' he asked.

'That's about it.'

'In which case…' And then, before he could say any more, she moved across the rug; he ex-haled a small sigh of relief and then he'd pulled her down next to him and he was kissing her. Kissing her as though their lives depended on it and in truth that was how it felt as need es-calated through her, her hands slipped under his T-shirt and she gasped at the wonder of fi-nally touching him.

'We need to get back to the villa,' he said raggedly. 'Before we get plastered across social media. And I don't think it's the castle they'll be interested in.'

She gave a half-hiccup of laughter and dazedly got to her feet. They quickly grabbed all their stuff, her easel, her sketchbook and the spades, before dusting the sand from themselves briskly and hurrying off.

The walk back seemed interminable, her whole body yearning, desperate, her calves aching as she tried to move faster up the dusty terracotta track.

Then they were inside the villa, dropped everything any which way, and headed to the bedroom.

'Thank God,' he said as they entered, and he was kissing her again, and now his hands were tugging at the sundress, and then her phone buzzed.

'Ignore it.'

She tugged it out of her pocket, about to switch it off, when an image of Stella filled the screen. Both their gazes fell to it and Adriana couldn't help it—the image of her sister's face triggered an instant reaction and she froze.

Unwanted memories streamed through her mind—of Steve, of the last time a man had kissed her, wanted her, made love to her. That was a man who had been fantasising about Stella, thinking of Stella.

No, no, no! Rob wasn't Steve.

No, but he was man who had wanted to

marry her sister, spend his life with her, sleep with her, have children with her.

But he never even went on a date with her.

But…it no longer mattered, panic swathed her, an insidious fear that she was being made a fool of yet again.

'Adriana?'

'I'm sorry… I…'

'It's OK. We don't have to do anything you don't want to do.' He moved away, his voice abrupt. 'Just give me a minute though.'

'I am so sorry, Rob.'

'It's OK. I would never want you to do anything you didn't want to. Or pretend…'

'No.' The word fell from her lips with vehemence. Because she could see more than confusion in his blue yes. She saw hurt and something she couldn't quite comprehend. 'I wasn't pretending.' How could he think that, why would he think that?

'You changed your mind.' He lifted a hand as if to take hers and then dropped it. 'That is OK.'

'No, it isn't. I mean, it is, but it's not that. I mean…' Oh, God, why couldn't she think straight? Probably because her body was on edge, roiling with frustration and hurting from the poisonous slew of memories. 'I did but I wasn't faking.' She took a deep breath. 'I'd like to explain.' Well, she wouldn't like to, but she knew if she didn't this would become something that could cause an ongoing problem. Because he didn't believe her even if she didn't understand why. And she wanted to soothe the hurt she could see shadow his blue eyes. 'But not here.'

He nodded. 'Come on. I know where we can go.'

CHAPTER ELEVEN

As they walked to the car Rob breathed in the flower-scented air and wondered if he even wanted to hear Adriana's explanation. Yet it was always better to know and face the truth. Even if it meant being hurt. Because better to know now if the attraction factor was fake on Adriana's side.

Yet could she have faked the kiss, the passion, the need? Stupid question—of course she could. Emily had, after all, taken him in completely.

Why shouldn't this be a rerun? Adriana wanted to marry him for the sake of Salvington—she had said herself she would do anything for Salvington. So why wouldn't she do what Emily had done? Lie back and think of… in Adriana's case, the splendour and beauty of her ancestral home?

As the thoughts streamed and whirled in

his mind, he forced them into abeyance and focused on the drive, followed the sat nav to his chosen destination—a glorious botanical garden, a place where he sensed it would be easier for them to speak, a setting where if it became too much, the beauty of the place, the warmth, the colours would help. Give them breathing space.

Once they'd parked they walked to the entrance, purchased tickets and entered.

'Is it all right if we walk for a bit?' she asked. 'Then talk? It'll give me a chance to gather my thoughts.'

He nodded and for a while they did exactly that, wandered the beautifully structured paths, took in the array of exotic plants, Azaleas and orchids from the Himalayas, Scottish heather, and a collection the placards informed them were cycads. They surveyed the thick trunks and the sprouting crown of large, stiff, dark green leaves.

Then onwards until they came to a massive lake. 'Shall we sit?' he asked, and she nodded.

'Yes. Thank you for bringing me here. I feel a bit more together. And I want to tell you, explain what happened back there.'

He tensed, tried to relax his shoulders, studied her face as she pushed her fringe away in the familiar impatient gesture.

'Go ahead,' he said. 'I'm listening.'

'I wasn't faking. I was worried *you* were.' Her voice was small now, small and sad and vulnerable.

Her words made his head swim. 'Me?' He could only hope utter incredulity could be housed in such a short syllable.

'I saw Stella's image on the screen and…'

Rob took a deep breath. 'I'm sorry. I don't understand.'

She looked toward the lake where Koi carp floated and occasionally gave a lazy jump. 'Stella is… Well, Stella is Stella—she is beautiful, smart, funny, and she does have that wow factor. If you put me and Stella next to each other any man would choose Stella, given the choice. When we saw her I panicked.'

'But why? I told you already I'm not remotely attracted to Stella.'

'But you were going to marry her. She was your first choice.'

He sensed he was on complicated terrain. 'Yes. But it wasn't a choice between her and you. Your offer wasn't on the table when Stella and I made our plans. What happened between us was between us. You and me.'

'I want to believe that.'

'Then why don't you?' He was trying to get it, he really was, but it didn't make sense to him. And he couldn't help but wonder if she was trying to spare his feelings in some way, find an excuse.

She twisted her hands together, looked around as if to take strength from their surroundings, the verdant greens and the bloom and the splash of the waterfall as it flowed smoothly into the blue waters of the lake. 'I told you that I had a serious boyfriend who I loved but he didn't love me. There was a bit more to it than that. I met Steve at a party, one that Stella dragged me to. It was a charity shindig and she was really insistent, so I went. Steve was there. He started talking to me and it was…nice. Extra-nice because it was unusual as he didn't seem to be interested in Stella. And at the end of the evening he asked me on a date.'

She said it as though she couldn't understand why and he wanted to say, But of course he would, why wouldn't he?

'And after that…he swept me off my feet. I mean, with hindsight I should have seen the cracks, but I didn't. He was very interested in meeting the family and sometimes we'd double-date with Stella. But he seemed to adore *me*. So I fell and I fell hard. Then one day I found a key at the back of one of his drawers—I was looking for a stamp or something. I wouldn't have given it a thought except there were some photos with the key. I wasn't snooping to start with, but I saw the top of a photo and I recognised Stella. Turned out all the photos were of her. I can still remember the coldness in the pit of my stomach as I tried to tell myself it was OK.'

He recognised that feeling all too well and he reached out to take her hand in his.

'Rightly or wrongly, then I did snoop. I found a locked shed at the bottom of the garden. It was…like a shrine to Stella.'

Jeez. He could only try to imagine how that must have felt, to walk in and see that.

'Massive photos of her everywhere, press cuttings, printed-out internet stories, glossy magazines. And a diary. Saying how he felt about her, talking about me, how every time he touched me he thought of Stella, fantasised about my sister. How he adored me as a sort of conduit, the closest he could ever come to her.'

Anger filled him, a desire to go and find Steve and make him see the error of his ways. 'What a creep…what a low-level, slimy waste of space. I wish… I wish I could have spared you that, I am so very sorry that he put you through that.'

'I haven't dated anyone since and today when I saw Stella's picture on the phone I… it all came back to me and I froze, all I could remember were those awful memories, the humiliation of it all and how I couldn't go through that again.'

'I get it.' Of course he did. He moved forward, squatted down in front of her, still holding her hand. 'I swear to you that the only person in my mind, the only person I was thinking of was you. That is the truth. I wish I could make you believe me. Because I know how horrible it is to go through what you did.' He hesitated but knew that he wanted to tell Adriana if sharing his own hurt would help her with hers, make her know that he understood her pain. 'Shall we walk whilst we talk?' he asked.

She nodded and he rose, pulling her gently up with him, kept her hand in his as they started to walk the cobbled paths lined with Portuguese tiles from centuries gone past.

'Emily was like Steve in a lot of ways,' he began. 'Her interest wasn't in me…it was in my wealth and position. With hindsight that should have been obvious, *I* should have seen the cracks. But I didn't. I believed her, believed she loved me for me, believed she was attracted to me. But she didn't and she wasn't. The whole thing was fake. She was still in love with her ex, who was in prison. But she wanted the glory of being a countess, and when I proposed she accepted. Then her ex came out of prison and she started seeing him. Faking it with me whilst seeing him. Eventually she got caught on camera and the proverbial hit the fan.' Her hand tightened around his and she moved closer to him, their steps completely in sync. 'She thought she could sweet talk me back, thought I'd forgive her, but I didn't. Suddenly I could see how fake it all was.' It had been a true eye opener and the worst of it was how sure she'd been that she could bring him round, lure him back in, so sure of her absolute power over him. A power he would never give a woman again. 'I told her it was over and she was furious.'

Adriana nodded. 'As though it were your fault.'

'Exactly.'

'Steve was like that. He couldn't see that he was at fault. It was as though he expected me to understand how he felt about Stella and actually be grateful that I was "the moon to her sun". He seemed surprised when I told him it was over.'

'That's how Emily was.' Her beautiful face had contorted with confusion and then when she realised her hold on him was truly broken she'd lost her temper. 'She said she'd make me pay and she did. She took her story to the press and she milked it for all it was worth. Tore me to shreds in the most humiliating way possible.' His skin still crawled at the memory. 'Emily discussed my prowess in the bedroom, or lack of.' In ways he wished he could eradicate. 'In one of her interviews she told the interviewer she'd lain back and thought of her ex. She also made it plain what a credulous fool I'd been, but somehow she did it in a way that made me look like an upper-class twit and she was wholesome and naïve and taken in. That somehow I'd tricked her, dazzled her with money but in the end true love had won through.'

'Even as she was pocketing the hefty fees from the press.'

'Yup. Got it in one.'

He kept his tone mocking, light and full of self-deprecation, braced himself for the pity that he would see in her grey eyes. But there was no pity, there was compassion and there was empathy—of course there was, because she understood implicitly what he had gone through just as he understood her pain.

But there was anger in her eyes too. 'I am so sorry, Rob. Sounds to me like she and Steve would have been a perfect match. Thank you for telling me and I understand now why you thought maybe I was faking. I wasn't.'

The last two words were simple and impossible to disbelieve.

'I believe you.'

'Good.' Now her face lit up in a smile so delightful that it almost hurt him to look at it, his chest squeezing with a warmth he didn't understand. She gazed into his eyes and he could see a tentative trust dawn. Then she leant over and brushed her lips against his, the sweetness, the hesitation, the sheer momentousness of the gesture blasting him with a wave of warmth and desire. She pulled away. 'Good,' she said again. 'Because I believe you too.'

'Good.' Now he pulled her back into his arms, oblivious of other tourists strolling past them. And he kissed her. Properly kissed her, savoured the taste of her, the scent of the flowers mingled with her vanilla shampoo creating a sensory miasma that dizzied him as she wrapped her arms around his neck, pressed her body against his in the language of yearning and need.

Until finally, as a reminder of where they were, a pointed cough broke the spell. They broke apart and she gave a gasp of laughter. 'I… What now?' she asked.

'Now? I think we need to go, get back to the villa. As fast as we can.'

'Let's go.'

They walked hand in hand, and as they walked the beauty of their surroundings made only the most distant impression on him, a sense of contrasting colours, the red of tiles on pagodas against the dark green fronds and bursts of colour from exotic flowers. A glimpse of two marble dogs that he vaguely recalled were mythical animals from the Orient, usually found guarding the entrance to temples.

They gathered pace, barely paused even when they spotted a flock of swans, pristine white, floating lazily on the lake, a stray peacock seen from the corner of his eye. All of this served as a mere backdrop to Adriana, a scene that preceded the sight of their destination. Finally they exited the gardens, made their way down the steep decline to the car park and he noticed almost mechanically that his fingers were shaking as he fumbled with the keys.

Once in the car he focused, resisted the urge to put his foot on the accelerator and speed all the way back. Deep breath and a quick smile at Adriana, who smiled back at him, a smile full of promise.

Then, with a muttered curse at every red light, a sense of disbelief as they got stuck behind the slowest lorry in the whole world, finally they were back at the villa.

They scrambled out of the car and raced inside straight to her bedroom, and instinct took over as he gathered her into his arms, revelled in the glorious rightness of the sensations, the taste, the smell, the feel of her against him. And this time, as he tumbled her back onto the bed, he knew there was nothing on this earth that would or could stop them.

CHAPTER TWELVE

ADRIANA OPENED HER eyes, aware of a hazy sense of wellbeing, of glorious, exhausted satiation. She kept her breathing steady, not wanting to disturb Rob, revelled in his arm flung over her chest, his breath warming her bare shoulder.

The previous hours had been magical in their beauty, the joy, the laughter, the intensity and the aftermath, and the idea that they could share this for ever seemed impossible to contemplate. Adriana didn't understand it, hadn't known it could be like this, knew now what Stella had meant, knew too that, like it or not, it would be hard not to let the wonder of this connection affect how she felt about wanting to marry him. Who wouldn't want this for the rest of her life?

Warning bells began to peal. Slow down. Perhaps her parents had started out with this level of attraction—it hadn't led to happiness. Rob had been honest about his attraction to Emily—but attraction could be faked, could change, die, wither, and so she must not let it taint any decision they came to.

But getting to know Rob better here in Portugal had shown her other good things. He'd been understanding of her need for privacy with her art and he'd been more than understanding about Steve. She felt a strange sense of warmth and lightness at having actually spoken about Steve, told the horrible truth to someone.

She'd told nobody, not a soul, unable to share the depths of her humiliation, endure the scourge of pity her tale of woe would evoke. But she hadn't seen pity in Rob's blue eyes, she'd seen empathy. And she understood why. When she thought of Emily her hands clenched into fists—at least her own humiliation had been private, not splashed across the papers.

She glanced sideways at Rob, momentarily distracted by the length of his dark eyelashes, which contrasted with the blondness of his hair. Hair spiked by sleep, his features more relaxed now but still craggy and well-defined. And a sense of optimism warmed her.

They had both endured pain and hurt because of love—maybe now they could forge a calm, contented union. Calm? Contented? Her hormones jeered—there had been nothing calm about last night. But that was attraction—that was separate from the day-to-day life and arrangements of a convenient relationship.

She shifted slightly and smiled a sleepy, happy smile just as he opened his eyes.

'Morning,' he said. 'That's a big smile.'

'I was thinking if we did get married how much fun it would be having you on tap, so to speak.'

He blinked sleep away. 'Feel free to turn me on any time you like.'

She gave a gurgle of laughter even as desire shivered through her, and then in one deft movement he swung her up so she straddled him and smiled the wickedest smile she'd ever seen. 'No time like the present,' he said.

An hour later they were entwined together in a tangle of sheets and, dropping a kiss on her shoulder, he sat up. 'You stay here and I will go and sort out breakfast, and then I think we should spend the day exploring. There's a town near by that I'd like to show you.'

'Sounds good.' Right now she suspected anything would sound good.

'Give me half an hour.'

It was more like an hour before the tantalising waft of coffee and croissants drifted into the bedroom, and as Adriana entered the kitchen it was to see the patio table set with a delicious array of food.

'I am ravenous,' she declared as she heaped her plate, then said. 'So where are we going?'

'It's a historic town, with a magnificent cathedral, beautiful churches, cobbled streets and lots of restaurants. And...something else I think you'll like.'

'Tell me.'

He shook his head. 'Nope. It's a surprise.'

Warmth touched her—no one had ever surprised her before. But Rob was surprising in more ways than one and her earlier optimism burgeoned inside her. They could make this work—they were building a base for a future together. Why would they need love when they had this? They liked each other, were forging a friendship, and on top of that they had attraction. Rob truly found her attractive. He was kind and civil and polite. They both needed to marry someone quickly, they both wanted a child, neither of them wanted love. This could work.

She took one last gulp of coffee. 'Then what are we waiting for? Let's go.'

Half an hour later they reached the bustling historic town, parked the car and started to wander through the winding streets that dipped up and down. Paused to browse the market stalls where fruit and flowers burst with colour and her fingers tingled to paint the scene. Poles were hung with bright bunches of dried chillies, wicker baskets of wares. Green guavas, a sample cut open to display the succulent pink inside, purple passionfruit with vivid yellow-orange flesh speckled with seeds sat alongside the more familiar bananas and grapes.

'I'm not even sure I know what some of those fruits are. Look at those—they look a bit like oddly shaped tomatoes.' She pointed at the small, round, ridged fruit that were varying shades of orange and red.

The stall owner overheard her question. 'They are called *pitanga*. They come here from Brazil. Try one. The more orange the fruit the more bittersweet…the darker it is the sweeter.'

As they walked on the scent of fruit mixed with the fresh bloom of flowers, the stalls all bustling, the sound of the vendors' chatter and cries floated on the balm of the breeze as they left the market behind. Walked along mosaic-tiled pathways towards an older part of town.

'We're nearly there,' he said. Now curiosity

did start to unfurl inside her, his smile looking so full of excitement, anticipation even, and she came to a halt.

'Where?' she asked.

'You'll have to wait and see.'

'OK.'

They walked a little further and then slowed down as they approached a long, winding cobbled street, ablaze with colour and artwork.

She paused, trying to assimilate it all. Realised that every door on the street hosted a different picture, a rectangle of individual artwork, the variety so immense it blew her mind.

'This is… I don't have words.'

'It's pretty awesome,' he said. 'I've never seen it—it wasn't here when I was a child but my parents mentioned it a few years back. This area was very run down, and the local government decided to try and change that. So local artists were all given the chance to paint the doors and now people come here specially to see this street, which has made it busy and so local businesses are thriving—cafes, shops and a couple of art galleries.'

As he spoke they walked down the street and she studied the different styles and techniques on display. 'That is so clever—I wish I could do it…the trompe l'oeil style. I'd love to do a massive canvas and manage to make it look three-dimensional. Manage to actually deceive the eye like this does. I mean, it feels as if I could walk straight into the garden. Oh, and this—this is brilliant, I love it.'

'Thank you.'

She whirled round to see a dark-haired woman smile at her. 'I am Isabella Rocha, the artist,' the woman explained.

'Oh, wow. That's amazing.' Adriana smiled at the woman. 'I love it, the colour, the lines, how alive it is. And how you've captured the detail.'

'Thank you. I think you must be Adriana.' Isabella Rocha turned to Rob. 'And you must be Rob.'

Adriana blinked as Rob said, 'Surprise. I did some research, saw that Ms Rocha was exhibiting here at a new gallery and I had the feeling you'd like her work. I thought you may want to meet her.'

'Call me Isabella, please. I also said I would give you a sneak preview of the exhibition,' she explained.

'That is really kind.'

'Well, yes, but I also persuaded Rob here to help a little with a charitable foundation I am part of, one that helps impoverished artists.'

Rob nodded acknowledgement and then smiled at Adriana. 'I'll meet you back here in an hour or so. I thought you may like to spend some time with Isabella on your own.' Warmth touched her because she knew why he was going; because she'd said her art was private to her and by going it would allow her to ask Isabella questions she may not feel comfortable doing with him there.

Adriana followed Isabella into the art gallery where she studied the paintings, listened to Isabella talk about her inspiration, where she had trained, how she worked. The whole experience was wonderful, and she couldn't believe an hour had gone past when the door opened and Rob came in.

'Thank you so much for showing me round. I feel truly privileged.'

'I enjoyed myself,' Isabella said. 'I was wondering…there's an opening party tonight. Would you like to attend? I am quite nervous. The owner is a celebrity, a famous actor. It would be nice to have a genuine fan of my work there. And a couple of friendly faces.'

Adriana's mind raced. A celebrity party? Nightmare scenario, surely. And yet…maybe it wasn't. For a start it would be the height of rudeness to decline, but more than that, this was a chance to see if she could put her money where her mouth was. See if she could fulfil Rob's faith in her. He'd said she could be a countess if she wanted to. Could hold her own in social situations—maybe this was the place to start.

'We'd love to,' she heard her voice say, and saw the look of surprise on Rob's face.

'Yes. Thank you,' he added. 'We would.'

'Marvellous.' Isabella took out a card and scribbled on the back of it. 'Here are the details. I look forward to seeing you both tonight.'

Once they had left, Adriana turned to Rob.

'She is amazing. Thank you so much for arranging that.'

'I'm glad you liked her. And I'm sorry about the party. I didn't know about that.'

She shook her head. 'Don't be sorry. I want to do this—maybe parties can be fun.' If you had the right person by your side, if you felt liked and desired. It occurred to her that this must be how Stella felt all the time and it was a way she had never felt before. 'But I need to go shopping.' She glanced at her watch. 'How about I meet you back here in, say, two hours? Is that OK?'

'That is fine. Unless you want some help.'

'Nope. I'm good.' Because now *she* wanted to surprise *him*.

Rob knotted his tie and gave his reflection a cursory glance. Everything in place, shirt properly buttoned, cuff links in, dinner jacket not a bad fit for a hired suit. He felt a sense of anticipation as he exited the bedroom and stood in the lounge area of the villa. Adriana had seemed pleased with her purchases and, whilst he had sensed that she was nervous about the upcoming party, he also believed her when she said she wanted to go.

'Here I am.'

He turned at the sound of her voice and his breath hitched in his throat. She looked absolutely stunning, and all he could do was stare at her. The dress was grey, her favoured colour, but it was a silvery grey and the material shimmered over her body. The spaghetti straps, the V-neck, the artfully placed necklace, the subtle slit down the side all combined to render him speechless, inspired a burning desire to tug her into the bedroom and remove the dress inch by tantalising inch.

'You like it?'

'I definitely, one hundred per cent like it.

You look incredible.' And it wasn't just the dress. Her hair shone and was pulled back in an elegant yet simple arrangement, so for once her face was in full view, no fringe in sight. Her grey eyes sparkled and she'd applied a light layer of make-up that emphasised the beauty of her lips and the classic slant of her cheekbones.

'You don't look so bad yourself,' she said, walking over to him, and again his lungs threatened to give up the ghost as she reached him and her sheer proximity dizzied him, the vanilla scent, the sheer kissability of her lips.

She smiled up at him, clearly read the desire in his eyes, and her own eyes darkened and she caught her lip in her teeth.

'Later,' she said on a whisper.

'Is that a promise?'

She smiled at him again, a smile that lit up her whole face as she grabbed his tie and pulled him towards her. 'It's a cast-iron guarantee.'

'I'll hold you to it.' He took her hand in his. 'And you're OK?'

'Yes. I'm nervous, but I'm OK. I've worked out that if I want to give this proposed marriage of ours a chance then I need to be able to do this, and today... I think I at least look the part.'

'You've nailed it. So let's go and wow the room.'

And Adriana did exactly that. From the moment they entered the room, a large, clean space with white walls on one side and cork walls on the other, ambiently lit with strategically placed lights that highlighted the different exhibitions, she didn't put an elegantly high-heeled foot wrong. And as he watched her chat about art, discuss local politics, and circulate whilst expertly managing to sample the canapes and hold a glass of champagne he wondered why on earth she had ever felt she couldn't do this. He was aware too that with each passing hour it became more likely that they would be able to conclude a successful negotiation, that this was most likely the woman he would spend the rest of his life with, would be the mother of his children.

A life where he managed the family estate and ran Easel, where she fulfilled all the roles and duties that befell a countess, and helped on the estate as well, a job he hoped she'd enjoy. A niggle of doubt touched him—would she enjoy that, working for Darrow where she didn't have the love of the place, the love that came of family pride and ancestry? But of course there would be their children, children he knew she would love and cherish. But children she was having now out of duty and, whilst he knew that wouldn't compromise her love for them, he was sure that if you took Salvington out of the equation Adriana may not choose to have a family right now. Wouldn't choose to have a family with him. Was this arrangement truly what she wanted, underneath it all?

He looked at her, so vital, so enthusiastic about Isabella Rocha's paintings. She was studying a picture now alongside the artist and another painter, asking questions, so focused, so alive.

And he saw she was in her element, her milieu, and he could no longer believe that art was simply a hobby for her; the equivalent of a morning run.

This was something truly important to her and a qualm struck him. He'd made a decision to keep his role in Easel alive, to do what he wanted to do alongside his duty. Why wasn't Adriana doing the same, and could he really believe she wouldn't come to regret prioritising Salvington over everything else?

'You OK?' Now she was by his side, looking up at him with a hint of concern.

'I'm fine. I've been enjoying watching you.' He smiled at her. 'I take it you're enjoying yourself.'

'Yes, I am. Isabella is incredible. And she's so kind as well—she doesn't mind me asking questions. She's inspirational.'

'Did you tell her you draw and paint yourself?'

'Of course not.' She looked aghast.

'Why not? Why don't you show her your work? See what she thinks.'

'No. There is no way I would impose on her good nature like that. Really there is no point.'

He frowned and she looked up at him and he could see panic in her grey eyes, cursed himself for being a fool. Talk about raining on her parade. 'That's fine,' he said lightly. 'It was just an idea.'

'Well, I've got a few ideas too for later,' she said. 'I think it's probably time to head back now, don't you?'

CHAPTER THIRTEEN

ADRIANA GLANCED ACROSS at Rob as they drove back to the villa, the darkness outside dotted with the occasional car light, the air thick with the sweet scent of hibiscus. His expression still held the same seriousness it had at the party and for a minute a sense of foreboding touched her.

'Is everything OK?' she asked, wondering suddenly if she'd done something wrong.

'Everything is fine.' The warmth of his voice reassured her. 'I've just been doing some thinking.'

'Sounds ominous,' she said, trying to keep her voice light.

'Nope. There's something I want to talk to you about. That's all.'

Talk was the last thing she'd been planning on doing. 'Can't it wait till morning?' she said softly. 'I thought we had other plans.'

This drew a smile. 'I hadn't forgotten, but I still want to talk first.'

The rest of the journey was completed in silence and once back at the villa she watched as he clicked the kettle on, made tea, which they carried to the kitchen table, sat down.

He'd shrugged off his jacket and now he unknotted his tie, and despite everything she felt the now all too familiar tug of desire in the pit of her tummy.

'So what do you want to talk about?' she said.

'You,' he said. 'Or more specifically your art.'

Adriana frowned. Whatever she'd expected, it hadn't been this. 'I told you. It's a hobby. I also told you I didn't like talking about it.'

'I know and I'm sorry, but we need to talk about it. Because I watched you tonight and earlier with Isabella. You were in your element and it sounded to me as though you really know what you are talking about, that this is a passion with you, something really important. So I don't understand why you don't want to talk about it. Why you haven't pursued it.'

'Because I don't want to,' she said, her voice flat.

'Because of Salvington?' he asked, gently.

'Because you feel you should work on the estate? At the expense of your art?'

'No! I told you, art is a hobby.' She was beginning to feel like a parrot.

'But are you sure you don't want it to be more than that?'

'Yes! I'm sure. Really.' She frowned. 'Why is it bothering you?'

'Because I don't want you to give up on something important to you because of Salvington. It doesn't have to be a choice. I want you to know that you can be a countess and an artist if that's what you want. I don't want your love of Salvington, or a sense of duty, to prevent you from pursuing this.' Warmth touched her at the fact that he cared, truly cared.

'This really matters to you.'

'Yes, it does.' He couldn't marry her if he knew she would regret it, knew he had to make her see the lesson he'd learnt himself. Even if that meant trusting her. Could he trust her? He could—he knew now that he could. Knew too that he wasn't getting through to her, could see it in the set of her chin, the fold of her arms. 'And it should matter to you as well. You only have one life, and you mustn't be bound by duty alone. I know how that feels.'

'I don't understand.'

'I told you how for my parents I was a miracle baby, and as such they were over-protective. But they weren't over-protective for *me*—it was the heir to Darrow who had to be kept safe at all costs.' Rob continued, 'I do understand their pride in our lineage—I do. And I do love Darrow. But...' He looked across at her and she could see the shadows in his eyes. 'But I don't feel it the way my parents do, or the way you do.'

'That's hardly surprising. I know your parents meant well but that isn't the way to engender love—you must have resented something that held you back from doing what you wanted to do.' How could a boy forced to do his duty, burdened and weighed down, not allowed to do anything he wanted in the name of that duty, made to fear he wasn't good enough, actually embrace it wholeheartedly? 'I love Salvington because I was allowed to forge my own connection with it, and maybe in times to come you will do that with Darrow.' And she vowed there and then to help him do just that.

'Perhaps. At the very least, I believe that it will be possible to do my duty to Darrow and have more than that. Find a balance. And I have found a way to do that.' He hesitated. 'I am telling you this in absolute confidence.'

'I understand.' She reached out and covered his hand with hers. 'I give you my word I won't break that confidence.'

'After Emily, when it had all gone so spectacularly wrong, I brokered a deal with my parents. They are getting old now and they want me to take over, which is fair enough. I asked for two years, two years in which I could go and do whatever I wanted. I thought it would give me a chance to get over Emily, so I promised after that time I would come back, settle down, take over the estate and marry suitably. They agreed.'

'So you went to the States and you discovered a different life.'

'Yes. As I've said, I was plain Rob Wilmington there. And I loved it.' Of course he had, after a life bound by duty, weighed down by his identity. 'The opportunity to discover what my life might have been like if I wasn't who I truly am was exhilarating. That's where I met Fleur and Jonathan, a couple in the house I was renting a room in. We became friends. One night we ended up talking and I got an idea. For a business. An idea for a website that offers people the chance to make their own websites—I know there are a few of those around but we came up with a way to make it super-easy and almost free. We had some added angles, ways of using social media, video clips, and a way to not only use stock clips and artwork but also make your own and market it. Anyway, the next day I thought, why not actually go for it?' He gave a half-laugh. 'I persuaded Fleur it could be a success and she agreed to it and Jonathan agreed to front it.'

'Because you wanted to keep out of it?'

'Yes. I didn't want anyone to work out who I really was—I wanted to be sure I'd achieved this as plain Rob Wilmington. And I did.' The simple words held a simple pride. 'Our partnership worked and we went for it and…it was amazing. In those two years we've got to the point where we are ready to launch Easel.' It was a good name, she thought. Combining the ease of use with the artistic side of it. 'For now I am going to keep out of the limelight, take a more background consultancy role. I don't want anyone to know of my involvement yet.' That was why he'd told no one, she realised— realised too what a leap of faith it was for him to trust her with this. 'Because I will keep my promise to my parents, I will learn the ropes on Darrow, I will be a good earl when my time comes and I will do my duty by my land, ready to pass on to the next generation.' She could hear pride in his voice, understood that he did love his land, but not exclusively. 'But then I will get a good estate manager and I will do both. I will be part of taking Easel global, to growing my company alongside working for Darrow.'

'That sounds…like a fantastic plan. I am truly happy for you.'

'Thank you, and if you wanted to play an active part in helping run Darrow of course you can. But my point is, you don't have to. If you want to pursue your art I would support you in any way I can. I understand how much you love Salvington but that love doesn't have to be exclusive—you can follow a different dream too.'

'I… I don't know if I can,' she said. Wasn't even sure if she wanted to.

'Why not?' he asked. 'I know it's a scary idea, doing something different, but I also know the joy it can bring. Building up Easel, there were times when we thought it would fail, times when I wondered if I could do it, if anyone would pay attention to my ideas without the glitter and shine my title and position gives them. But… I believed in my idea, and that belief got me through the doubts.'

'Maybe that's it, then. I don't believe.'

He frowned. 'Truly? You don't believe your work is good?' He looked at her as if she were a puzzle he was trying to unlock. And whilst the thought unnerved her, the idea that he was interested, that he cared, still warmed her.

Adriana sighed, cradled her mug in her hands and gave the question some thought. 'I... I don't know. Sometimes I think it is awful, rank amateur stuff that a child of five could do better, and other times, occasionally, I think it's OK. But mostly I try not to analyse it because I don't want to put myself off doing it.'

'But why not show someone? Your family? Why keep it a secret?'

'Because I can't bear for something precious to me to be destroyed,' she said softly. Knew Rob deserved a real explanation, deserved the truth after what he'd shared with her and because he did truly care, believed it was important.

'Tell me,' he said softly.

'When I first started drawing it really was a hobby, but I soon realised how much I loved it and that's when I knew I needed to keep it to myself. You see, my father...' She paused, twisted her hands together, and then in a deft movement reached up and let her hair out of its bun, ran her hands through it and for the first time in days allowed her fringe to hide her eyes. 'My father…he blamed me for all the problems with Salvington. My parents were told I was a boy at the gender scan— they weren't as sophisticated in those days, I suppose, and there is always some margin for error. Anyway, they believed I was the son and heir. I wasn't. Even worse than that, my mother developed endometritis after me and, rightly or wrongly, my father blamed me for that as well. Well, blamed me and my mother, really. The bottom line is he has always loathed the sight of me.'

'I had no idea—that is appalling.'

She shrugged. 'I sort of get it. I mean, I know it is completely wrong but his love for Salvington isn't rational, any more than perhaps your parents' is for Darrow. But your parents got what they wanted—an heir. My father didn't. He has never blamed Stella—he adores her. No matter what she did. It's not her fault and I know she has tried to show him that she isn't perfect but to him she can do no wrong. But me—he takes any opportunity to show his dislike. So as a child I learnt the best thing to do was for me to keep out of sight. That protected our mother. I mean, he never hurt us physically but…'

'Words can be weapons too,' he said. 'So you didn't tell him about your art because you knew he'd tear it to pieces, tell you you had no talent. I'm guessing too that if he has spent your whole life putting you down it's hard for you to believe in yourself. Even more so when it is something so important to you.' He leaned forward now, took her hands in his, and his clasp made her feel safe. 'You said you "sort of" get it. Well, I don't, and I don't think you should either. The way your father has treated you…it's wrong, Adriana. Truly wrong—it makes my blood boil with anger. It is unfair, unwarranted, unjustified and you did not deserve it. Now you've told me this it makes me admire you even more, for who you are despite what you've been through. And it makes me even more convinced that you should take your art further. Though I truly understand why you haven't.'

'Thank you. I feel…lighter. Maybe I can pluck up the courage to think about doing something more with my art.'

'Would you show me?' he asked and then immediately shook his head. 'Sorry. Forget that. I have no right to ask that.'

'Yes, you do. But it feels unfair to show

you—if it is totally pants I don't want you to have to tell me.'

He shook his head. 'I think lots of famous artists' work is pants,' he said. 'That's the beauty of art—it is an opinion. I wanted to see it because it's important to you, not to judge it.'

Adriana took a deep breath, knew that Rob had entrusted her with his secret, knew she could trust him not to hurt her feelings, knew too that if her work was rank and amateur he would be the best person to break it to her.

'I don't have much with me, only the sketch I did on the beach and a few bits that were in my portfolio.' She got to her feet. 'I'll go and get them.'

A few minutes later she entered the room, her heart pounding in her ribcage. This was the first time she'd ever shown anyone anything she had created and her nerves fluttered and twisted as she handed the sketchbook over.

He took it, gave her a reassuring smile, and she forced herself to keep her gaze on him, wanted to see his reaction, wanted the unvarnished truth.

His face remained smooth as he studied the sketches. The unfinished one of the beach and some others, a drawing of woodland, a field of flowers... 'I used the sketches as a basis for some paintings.' She scrolled down her phone and found the woodland painting. He took the phone, studied the painting and then looked up at her.

'I think they're amazing,' he said. 'There's something about them, a way you have of capturing a mood, or a moment in time. I think for authors it's called having a "unique voice", and you have something. I know I've only seen a sample of your sketches, but when we get back I'd love to see more and I'd love to see the paintings. And I think you should do something with this, Adriana. I do.'

A surge of happiness washed over her, because she knew he wouldn't say that, wouldn't let her risk making a fool of herself by showing Isabella or anyone else if they were rubbish.

'Thank you.' She didn't know what else to say—instead she moved over and leant down to kiss his cheek. 'Really.'

In an instant he'd tugged her down onto his lap.

'Thank you for showing me. For trusting me with something so precious to you.'

They sat in a comfortable, warm silence for a while, and then she rose and smiled down at him. 'I think I have a promise to keep and right now I could use some help taking this dress off.'

'Then I'm your man,' he said.

The words seemed to resonate round her head. Her man. The idea was heady enough to make her dizzy.

CHAPTER FOURTEEN

ROB PUT THE kettle on, whistled as he scooped coffee into the cafetiere and cracked some eggs into a bowl. Today he was opting for a break-fast of omelettes served with fresh bread. He chopped the green peppers he'd bought at the market early that morning and smiled as he recalled the rest of his purchases and arrange-ments.

He watched the onions sizzle in the pan and switched off the potatoes he'd brought to a boil. As he did so his mind revolved around his plans and his smile widened as he turned to see Adriana enter. In one hand was a towel she used to dry the glossy brown hair.

'Good morning.'

She glanced at her watch. 'It's barely still morning,' she said. 'Why didn't you wake me up?'

'You looked too beautiful lying there asleep.'

And he'd had things to do. 'So I went to the market, picked up some provisions and, *voilá*.'

'It smells amazing.' She poured water into the cafetiere. 'What shall we do today?'

'I have a plan. I think we should go in the cable car up the mountain and then we can toboggan back down again.'

'Sounds like fun.'

'I also thought if you want to take a sketchbook you can sit and draw the cathedral and I can catch up with some paperwork for Easel.'

'Better and better.' She grinned at him. 'Life is easier without secrets.'

A leisurely hour later and they were in the surprisingly short queue for the cable cars, but instead of keeping his eye on the blue cars as they made their jaunty way up and down the mountain he found himself watching Adriana. The way her eyes scanned her surroundings, the interest that lit the grey depths, and he realised how much he'd learnt about her, knew she was thinking now about how she would draw or paint the scene, how she would capture the glint of blue, the wisp of white cloud in the sky.

So much made sense—her dislike of social situations, her fear she wasn't good enough, her assumption that her sister was better than she was. All down to her father. He suppressed the quick surge of anger, told himself there was no place for it now. Lord Salvington was an ill man and whilst that didn't excuse his behaviour it certainly precluded Rob giving him a piece of his mind.

A cable car came to a stop and a few minutes later they were aboard, lucky enough to have the car to themselves. They sat opposite each other, hands clasped, as the car glided upwards.

'Look at that,' she said as she gazed out, and his gaze followed hers. Took in the stretch of red rooftops, a vivid contrast to the whitewashed walls of the houses, glimpsed the vibrant colours of people's gardens and the steep downward sweep of ravine gorges. 'The people look so tiny, it's almost like looking at a play world.'

At the end of the twenty-minute ride they reached the summit. 'I thought we could stroll along to the church first.' It was a place he thought she would like but he also needed to kill time, couldn't take her back to the villa until dusk.

'Sure.'

They walked along the cobbled paths, past the start point of the toboggan ride, down some stairs and then up another path that meandered between green hedges. Until they reached the church and she came to a halt.

'Oh. That's not how I imagined it would be.' He knew what she meant. The church was a symmetrical structure with white walls outlined in black, with large windows embedded in the walls.

'I read that the façade has a "baroque pediment",' he said, and she gave him a quick glance.

'Anything else you can tell me?'

'Yup. Originally there was a chapel built here in 1470 by someone called Adam, and Adam and his twin sister, Eva, were apparently the first children born on Madeira. This church, though, was built in the 1740s, then an earthquake damaged it, and then it was rebuilt and consecrated in 1818.'

'Anything else?'

He pointed to the stairs that led to the church. 'There are seventy-four of them.'

'Have you made that up?'

'Nope.' He grinned at her. 'Bet I'm right and if I am I get to claim a kiss whenever I want.'

'Seems like a win-win deal to me. Let's go.'

'Seventy-two…seventy-three…seventy-four!' he said in a tone of exaggerated triumph and she gave a small chuckle. They stood and looked at the imposing outside of the building for a moment. 'Shall we go in?'

'Definitely.' She gave him a sideways glance. 'I have the feeling there's lots to see inside and that you know all about it.'

'Correct. If we go inside we can see the tomb of Karl the First. He was the last Emperor of Austria, and when he was forced to cede his position he was exiled here, where he died. He was only thirty-four.'

'That's sad,' she said softly. 'He had to leave the place he loved, his home and give up something integral to his identity, to his being. Maybe it's no wonder he died young.'

'I read that his heart is in Switzerland but the rest of his body is in here.'

They entered the church and looked around the ornate interior, stood in front of a statue of the Virgin in a silver tabernacle.

'Legend says a shepherdess was given the statue centuries ago and lots of miracles occurred because of it. Also the main festival of the church, the Assunção de Maria, is held on August the 15th annually. It's a place of pilgrimage and those coming here often climb those seventy-four steps outside on their knees.'

She glanced at him and now there was definite speculation in her eyes. 'All of this is genuinely interesting, but I can't help feeling you had some ulterior motive in finding all this out. In fact, why do I have the feeling you know something I don't know?'

'I have no idea,' he said blandly, even as he glanced at his watch, checked the time, mentally went through the preparations for later on.

'Hmm. I do realise that that isn't really an answer.'

'How about we go and check out the toboggans?' he suggested. As they left the church and headed back along the path he realised how comfortable she was to be with—the silences were easy not awkward, both of them content to walk hand in hand and soak in the sun and scenery until they arrived.

As they waited in the queue she glanced up at him. 'So are you also a font of all knowledge on the toboggans?' she asked.

'Absolutely. I wanted today to be…special so I did all the research.'

Standing on tiptoe she brushed her lips against his cheek. 'Thank you. So tell me what you found out.'

'The toboggans are made of wicker and wood, eucalyptus wood to be precise. They run on greased slats, the grease used is tallow and there are ropes to help the drivers steer the toboggans. The drivers drive in pairs and they all wear white trousers, white shirts and straw hats with a black ribbon. Oh, and specially soled boots as well.'

'How fast do they go?'

'Anywhere up to thirty miles per hour. So it should be exhilarating.'

'Oh, we're about to find out.'

They climbed into the basket car and a few minutes later they were off, the two drivers expertly steering the toboggan. It was definitely exhilarating as they swooped and swerved downward, the scenery whizzing past as they both braced themselves.

'They are going to need to stop at the junction! How...?'

'I think that's where the boots come in—they help them brake,' he said as the car came to a surprisingly smooth stop, before restarting the journey.

'I love this,' she said and when he saw her smile, saw the graceful lift of her hand to hold her hair off her face, he felt a sudden thrill of anticipation for the evening ahead. But first they disembarked from the toboggan and elected to walk down to the city, holding hands as they navigated the steeply inclined back. Once there they wandered the cobbled paths, found a small restaurant where they ate spaghetti cooked in a Chouriço sauce before moving on to a café near the cathedral where Adriana sketched the simple façade of the building with its Gothic archways, and Rob focused on the Easel launch.

Then a quick glance at his watch, a hurried message to check everything was in place and then he said, 'Are you ready to head back now?'

'Sure.' She smiled at him. 'I've had a lovely day.'

'So have I.' As he looked at her, a small warning bell pealed at the back of his mind. One that he pushed away. There was no *need* for alarm. This was all going according to plan. He and Adriana had come here to Madeira to make sure they got on, make sure they liked each other enough to commit to a marriage.

So enjoying time together was a good thing. The attraction was a good thing. All ticks on a criteria list for a marriage of convenience. And he reassured himself he didn't feel the same way about Adriana as he had about Emily. There was no sense of agony, no fear of loss, no pangs of jealousy or hour upon hour spent trying to decide the best way to entertain her, or please her.

'Then let's go,' he said, a small smile on his lips as he anticipated her reaction once they got back.

Adriana glanced across at Rob, wondered what was going through his head, knew he wouldn't tell her but knew too it was nothing to worry about. They'd shared their secrets now, confided in each other, and that felt good. So she leant her head back and watched the scenery go by, felt the warm evening breeze ruffle her hair, braced herself against the now familiar dips and inclines of the roads.

Then they were back and as she climbed out of the car she sensed that something was different. Following him into the house, she glanced round, couldn't see anything amiss, and then she followed him across the lounge as he pulled open the sliding doors and she gave a small gasp.

The patio had been transformed. Fairy lights twinkled in a cascade of illumination that cast light and shadows over the mosaic tiles, lit up the potted plants and the fronded trees and cast enough light to show the dark blue of the waves that lapped and frothed down below.

The circular table had a white damask cloth over it with a centrepiece of blooming flowers that filled the air with a floral scent that she knew would be embedded in her memory for ever along with the vibrancy of colour and light. A silver wine cooler held champagne and silver platters with covered dishes were artfully scattered.

'It's beautiful,' she breathed as he walked forward and pulled out a chair for her to sit on.

It was then that she saw there was a package next to her plate, a long rectangular shape encased in thick gold paper and tied up with a pretty bow.

'It's for you,' he said.

'For me?' Carefully Adriana opened the beautifully wrapped parcel. 'Thank you.' Inside the wrapping there was a box of artist's pencils, ones she recognised as being top-notch, not just because of their price tag but also because of their name.

He smiled. 'I cheated a little. I asked Isabella for a recommendation. Have a look inside.'

She lifted the lid and then froze. Nestled amongst the pencils was a jewellery box. With trembling fingers she opened it, stared down at the ring inside, a ring that her artist's mind could see was a burst of colour that matched the flowers in the centrepiece, a detail that for some reason made her blink back a tear.

'Adriana, will you marry me?'

She nodded and he reached over, took the ring and carefully slid it onto the ring finger of her left hand. 'I promise to always try to make sure our marriage is a happy one.'

The words were full of seriousness and yet somewhere deep down Adriana felt a pang of sadness, one she quelled instantly. There was no reason for sadness—this was what she wanted. She had known from the start their marriage was a deal, one that would be protected by a prenup agreement. But that didn't mean they couldn't broker a happy marriage. A marriage that could save Salvington *and* provide them with a union that would be a happy one. With a man she liked, a man she respected and a man she desired. That was enough—of course it was.

'And so do I,' she said, and if her smile held a hint of sadness she could only hope he didn't see it.

'And here we have a selection of tapas,' he said. 'I ordered them in, and there are even numbers of them so we can share them equally, so you definitely don't miss out on anything.'

Now her smile was genuine and as he lifted

the plates and showed her the delicious dishes, he told her exactly what each one was, the *polvo à galega*, octopus and potatoes cooked with garlic and paprika, oysters served with lemon juice, *peixinhos da horta*—green beans fried in a tempura batter—and *gambas na frigideira*—prawns fried in a special sauce of whisky, port wine with garlic and sweet peppers. Then he opened the champagne and as they ate and drank, dusk turned to night and she looked down at her engagement ring as it glittered in the moonlight.

And seemed to send her a message: this is enough. Be content.

CHAPTER FIFTEEN

A week later

ROB LOOKED AROUND his annexe at Darrow, noted the evidence of Adriana everywhere, small, subtle reminders that he was engaged, that she was definitely now a part of his life on the estate. A stray barrette, an upturned book, a piece of paper, entitled *Things You Need to Do*—things she wanted him to do before their engagement announcement and party. They'd decided to hold a small party at Darrow itself, not too large, as the wedding itself would be a massive affair, so the engagement party would be low-key, just family and close friends. Plus Adriana was keen to announce the engagement and then get married as soon as possible. Whilst her father was stable, he still wasn't recovering as quickly as the doctors had hoped, still seemed lethargic and fragile. Though news of the engagement had definitely sparked a positive reaction and he knew Adriana hoped that the official announcement would bolster that.

His gaze went back to the to-do list; it reminded him of things on his own list. He needed to sort out the prenup agreement, but he was unsure why he kept putting it off. It was important to ensure that Adriana couldn't get sole custody of his heir, as long as the prenup protected her as well—they'd agreed that at the outset. Difficult to believe how short a time ago that was. Yet reluctance still touched him, one he must overcome. But in the meantime there was something he could do—he could sort out a health check for himself. The other thing they'd discussed.

He'd just dropped his phone back in his pocket when there was a knock at the door and he looked up to see Adriana, rose to his feet, knew the smile on his face was ridiculously wide, considering he'd seen her only the previous day.

'Was I expecting you?' he asked.

'No, and I haven't come here to check on the to-do list either,' she said with a grin, no doubt clocking his guilty glance towards it. 'I've come to take you on a picnic. I'd like you to show me round Darrow, seeing as I'm going to help you run it.'

'OK. But would you like to meet the estate manager or…?'

'Nope, I want you to show me.'

He looked at her, wondered why he had the feeling there was some ulterior motive to the request.

'Take me to your favourite place on Darrow. And we can eat there. And then I'd like to maybe see the Woodlands. It's a lovely day after all.'

It truly was. The sun shone and the smell of freshly mown grass pervaded the air as they walked alongside freshly ploughed fields until they reached a woodland glade. And somehow walking with Adriana, answering her questions about the farming done on the land, discussing eco methods, he felt a sudden muted pride in his land.

'I think there are so many things you could do here. There are places that you could preserve for wildlife, there are grants you can get to help with that. And I know you have the capacity to grow market produce; you could start a farmers' market. One day perhaps it would even be worth having an area set aside for the public, you could have a play area and a small farm for children to visit, with pony rides and…' She broke off. 'But right now I know what I'd like to do.'

'What?'

She narrowed her eyes as she looked towards the glade. 'Climb that tree over there. And you could climb the one next to it. What do you think?'

'You want to climb trees?'

'Yes,' she said. 'I told you that when I was a child I spent hours exploring Salvington, roaming the land, climbing trees, building shelters and all the stuff we've just been talking about that is really important, but so is forming a connection with the estate, and I thought today…maybe we could start doing that. Together. Because I'd like to love Darrow as well. And I'd like our children to feel a connection to their land, but I'd like us to teach them that in a way that you weren't taught. That way they won't feel like you did, won't feel burdened or weighed down with responsibility. But to teach a connection you have to have a connection. Does that make sense or do you think I've run mad?'

'No. That makes sense.' But he could still see worry on her face and reached out to smooth the crease from her forehead. 'What's wrong?'

'I don't want you to think that I was trivialising all the things we were talking about, about farming methods and crops and eco management. They are so important, the nuts and bolts of running an estate. And your father was right to teach you that. I also know how much I have to learn about those nuts and bolts.'

'I don't think you are trivialising anything. You're saying that having a connection to your land makes you want to learn how to look after it to the best of your ability. In the same way I have a connection to Easel because I created it, spent blood, sweat and tears getting the funding, getting it right, and now I will always do all I can to take it forward.'

'Yes, and I believe you can feel like that about Darrow as well.'

'I'd like to try,' he said. And he would; as he looked at her now, seeing the serious look on her face lighten as her lips turned up in a smile, his chest seemed to squeeze tight. 'So let's start. I'll race you to the top.'

And as he climbed, figured out which branch could take his weight, trusted his instincts to help him alight the sturdy breadth and height of the tree he felt a sudden sense of exhilaration, akin to how he felt when ice skating, and when he'd reached as high as was safe to go and looked down he had a boyish urge to proclaim himself King of the Castle. He saw Adriana in the next tree seated on a sturdy branch, one hand resting on the trunk, her legs swinging.

'This is amazing,' he said.

'I know. I used to spend hours in my favourite tree with a book and some snacks. Maybe when we have kids we can build them a tree house—that was always one of my dreams. My father would never have helped me do it but I'd love us to help our children.'

He could hear the wistfulness in her voice. 'Deal,' he said. He could picture it now, Adriana and himself helping an exuberant little boy and a determined little girl lay some planks. 'I promise that I will be a better father than either of ours.' He shook his head. 'Though that's not setting the bar that high, I know. So how about I will be the very best father I know how to be?'

'I know you will and I truly believe you will be a great father.'

He glanced across at her. 'How is your father?'

'Stable but still frail.' She sighed. 'I think

he is glad about our marriage, but I know he wishes it were Stella. He is still refusing to see her. So she won't come to the engagement party.' Another sigh and then a small shake of her head, as though to dislodge thoughts of her family. 'So where shall we have our picnic?'

'There's a river near here. Let's eat next to it and then paddle.'

'Sounds perfect.'

And it did; for a moment foreboding touched him. Though he wasn't sure why. After all, he had it all, didn't he? He'd found the perfect wife for a convenient marriage. 'Oh and whilst I remember we need to sort out some of the legal side of things before the engagement announcement.' He forced himself to continue. 'Like the prenup,'

The words acted like a cloud that obscured the sun, though he knew that was only in his imagination, knew if he hadn't said it now he would never have said it. Would have let the dream of the perfect family take over from the reality. And so what if they signed a prenup? It wouldn't stop them from building a tree house for their children, or being a happy family.

Yet as he descended the tree he knew some of the exhilaration of the day had seeped away.

* * *

A few days later and Rob stared across the desk at the man who had just delivered such devastating news, in such a clinical fashion. 'I see,' he said.

'I'm sorry, Mr Wilmington. But it isn't all bad news—as I said…'

Rob nodded. 'I fully understand the situation. I have a low sperm count. Conceiving a baby may take a lot of time. There are also possible treatments but no guarantees.' A completely uncharacteristic sense of anger threatened, urged him to tip the fancy desk over, lean across and shake the consultant till his teeth rattled.

But of course he didn't—it wasn't this man's fault.

'Thank you. I'll be in touch.'

It took all his iron will to allow him to rise from his seat unhurriedly to leave the room at his usual pace, though once out on the street he started to walk faster, his brain churning, analysing, trying to find a way out, a solution.

Tried to fight off the bleak knowledge that there wasn't one. That there was no way he could now marry Adriana. The knowledge was like a punch to the solar plexus and the pain spread through his body, through his heart, his very soul.

Enough.

This reaction was extreme and yet he felt clammy, ill…sick. Perhaps it was a reaction to the diagnosis—that would make more sense. After all, getting an heir would now be more complicated than he'd foreseen, and his situation could be a rerun of his own parents' quest. And if he failed so did the line of Darrow. Yet those facts didn't seem to be having an impact; all he could think of was the immediate consequence: he could not marry Adriana.

He tried to focus on the positives—at least he had found out now, before the marriage, before the preparations were truly underway. But that lining was so thin it may as well be a near-invisible glimmer of silver.

He could not marry Adriana.

And that thought was clouding everything, casting a shadow, causing a deep, raw pain that he couldn't seem to wrestle under control.

He forced himself to stop, saw that he was outside a café, forced himself to go and order a coffee, hoped the scorching hot caffeine would somehow allow him to think beyond the pounding echo of *You cannot marry Adriana*.

Because he had to think, to see if there was a solution, a way.

Cradling the coffee cup, he resumed walking, oblivious of the London crowds that thronged the pavements. He had to get a grip—why was he feeling like this? Yes, it was unfortunate, but it wasn't the end of the world. When Stella had pulled out of their agreement it hadn't mattered apart from a sense of aggrieved inconvenience.

His conversation with Adriana echoed in his head.

'You had feelings for her?'

The words had made him pause.

'I liked her, but I suppose that's the beauty of an arranged marriage—it is a business arrangement first and foremost. So I am upset in the same way I would be if a deal fell through. It's an...'

'Inconvenience?' she'd offered. *'And you'll be looking for a new partner forthwith?'*

'Yes.'

The words mocked him now, because this wasn't an inconvenience, this was...devastating, the knowledge he no longer had a future with Adriana, and now images streamed through his mind. Her laugh, her smile, waking up with her wrapped in his arms, her hair tickling his chest, his cheek, her arm flung over him. Listening to her, her listening to him, the way she pushed her fringe off her face, the small frown, the infectious laugh, her scent, her taste…the life they'd planned together.

A life with a brood of children.

All over.

A burn of pain scalded his hand and he realised he'd inadvertently crushed the coffee cup and allowed the liquid to spill over him.

Enough. He had to get himself under control and he had to admit to himself that somehow the unthinkable had happened. He loved Adriana.

And there was nothing he could do about it. Because he also remembered her other words,

'I love Salvington, and the risk is worth it to me. I want my children to have the chance to explore the land and places that I roamed as a child. I want to keep Salvington in the Morrison family, to see it prosper and grow. I want to be part of that. I will do anything I can do to make that happen.'

That was what mattered to her. She'd spoken of her connection to her land, and he knew the most important thing in the world to her was to try and save it. That meant the best thing he could do for the woman he loved was to pull out of this agreement and never let her know of his love.

Because he knew that would tear her in two, that she would already feel compassion for him because of the fertility issues he faced, and if she knew how he felt about her that would only deepen the compassion and cause her conflict. What if she loved him too? The question whispered at the back of his mind.

Then, even then, their marriage couldn't work. He wouldn't let her choose the transience of love over what mattered most to her. Wouldn't let their marriage become an echo of her own parents'.

He clenched his hands into fists. The bleakness intensified as he realised exactly what this meant. That he'd never kiss her again, never wake up next to her, never watch her push her fringe off her forehead, never...

Never happening. Adriana wanted to marry him for a child, an heir, a chance to save Salvington. That had been the cornerstone of negotiation, the only reason she'd approached him, the only reason she'd contemplated marrying him. With or without love, without that stone the whole edifice collapsed in a cloud of debris and dust. That was the stark truth and he knew exactly what he had to do and he'd do it. Man up and do his duty, do the right thing. For her.

He glanced at his watch—he was due to meet her in his London flat in half an hour. Ironically enough to discuss the prenup. No need for that now.

Adriana let herself into Rob's London flat. She hadn't been here before but he'd said she should have a key. In case she was doing 'wedding things' in London and needed a place to have a cup of tea.

She pushed the door of the lounge open and entered, saw that he was sitting at his desk.

'Rob?'

He turned and she halted at his expression. He looked…hard, his expression withdrawn, the set of his lips grim. As though he'd steeled himself to an unpleasant task. She knew the prenup was a sensitive subject but surely it didn't warrant this.

'What's wrong?' She headed forward, hands outstretched as he rose to his feet, kept his own hands by his sides, the distance on his face, in his body language, the tension in his legs and shoulders and jaw absolute. He gestured to a chair, the movement awkward as though he was directing his arm with an effort.

She sat, perched on the edge of the chair, hands clasped on her knees as she waited.

'There is no easy way to say this. The deal is off the table. I can't marry you.'

Shock froze her. 'Why not?'

'I went for a full health check. Like I said we should both do before the wedding. I figured I'd go first.'

Panic escalated as nightmare scenarios crossed her mind.

'It turns out I have a very low sperm count.'

Her first reaction was sheer relief, that he wasn't dying, wasn't stricken with a life-threatening disease. But then came understanding as she put the statements together. *Low sperm count.* Adriana stared at him as the fact lodged in her brain, nudged the first domino and sent the whole lot tumbling down, crushing hopes and dreams, obliterating engagement-party plans and wedding-venue arrangements. *Can't marry you.*

Desperately she tried to stem the crash, reverse the domino effect. 'But that doesn't mean it's impossible for you to have a child. For us to have a child.'

'No. But it's very unlikely to happen quickly. Timing is everything for you.' She stared at him, hands twisting in her lap, nails in her palms as she forced her mind to think. 'You told me that your father's recovery is slower than you'd like. So logically there is no choice but to call the marriage off. Dissolve the partnership.'

'Without discussion?'

'There isn't anything to discuss.'

'There must be something to discuss. How can you sit there like that? And talk about logic? Don't you care?' He flinched at that and she rose, moved towards him. 'This is me. This is us. We had a future planned. You must feel something, that this is more than just an inconvenience. Please, Rob. I am not your parents. You don't have to man up and only think about the earldom.'

Finally his body sagged a little, the awful tension lessened its taut hold, and now he too rose, moved towards her. 'I do care, Adriana. And I'm not thinking about the earldom. I am thinking about you, about us, about our agreement.' He took her hands in his and she knew with awful finality that it was the last time he'd do so. The last time she'd feel his touch. 'We did have a plan. And that plan centred around having a family. The whole reason you wanted this marriage was to give yourself a chance to have a son, to save Salvington.'

Oh, God. He was right.

His voice was gentle now. 'Your home, your place, your land. You told me you would do anything to save it, asked me to imagine a scenario where your father dies and you know you did not do everything you could to save Salvington, how you would feel to see the diggers wrench up the earth and soil of a place you love. Desecrate it. So I have imagined that. Imagined us married, trying for a baby and trying for a baby whilst your father's health hangs in the balance. It's not your father I am thinking about—it's you. What that would do to you. To us. I couldn't bear to watch your unhappiness and know that I am the cause. Don't want our marriage to go the way of your parents'. Or mine.'

She bit her lip. What to do about her father, about the situation with Salvington? And more importantly, what about Rob? What must this news have done to him?

'What about you? I won't desert you because you…'

'Can no longer provide you with what you need?' he said. 'Yes, you can. You are not deserting me. That was always the point of our marriage—it was a partnership based on a provision of mutual benefits. I can't give you what you need.'

'But…' She took a deep breath. Now it was sinking in and she could only imagine how he must feel, given that his whole life he had known it was his duty to carry on the line of Darrow, to have an heir. Now that was no longer straightforward and the weight of responsibility must be heavier than before. The anxiety of failure. 'Forget about us for a moment. This is a massive shock. You must be reeling from it.'

'Things happen. There is a chance I will have a child, but possibly not a large family unless there is a treatment.' Now she heard the slight crack in his voice. Knew how much that would hurt. There was a chance he would end up having an only child, just as he had been, a child who would bear the whole burden of familial expectations. He stepped back now and she could see his withdrawal. 'But all this is for me to manage.'

For him to manage. With another woman. The idea took her breath away, as a deep, visceral pain twisted inside her. Enough. There should be no pain, no hurt. That was supposedly the beauty of their arrangement. No reason to feel pain.

This was an agreement, a deal, exactly what they'd discussed just weeks before. But that had been then, before they had got to know each other, before she'd learnt so much about him, the way he smiled, that strong sense of duty, countered by a sense of humour and an ability to make her laugh, before she'd discovered he cared about her, before she'd confided in him about Steve, about painting, about the way her father had treated her all her life. Before he'd confided in her, before they'd climbed trees together, goddamn it, before they'd gone tobogganing. Before they'd made love, before she'd got used to waking up next to him… Her brain caught up with the slipstream of thoughts, focused on the word, the taboo. Love. They had made love because she loved him. Had fallen for him, heart, body and soul. She loved him.

The realisation froze her, caused her skin to come out in a cold, clammy sheen of panic. How had this happened, how had she let him find a way under her skin, into her heart? She'd been so sure love would not come into play, sure she was immune from even the slightest possibility. Because she'd only ever approached him for Salvington's sake.

Or maybe that wasn't true, maybe that stupid crush from years ago had never abated, maybe that was all this still was, some sort of foolish infatuation.

But right now she couldn't think straight, knew she had to keep this from him at all costs. With her heart aching, she reached up and slipped the barrettes from her hair, those barrettes he'd given her and she'd worn like a talisman since. But now she didn't want him to read her eyes, couldn't bear to see the pity in his if he guessed, and there would be pity because he would know exactly how she felt. He'd loved Emily and Emily hadn't loved him back. But in his case he'd been duped. Rob had never lied to her, never led her on, had been more than clear love was never on the table, never a possibility.

But then, she'd been so sure of that herself; for a mad moment she wondered if there was any way that his take on it all had changed, that he had fallen in love with her. And an impulse nearly overcame her—to tell him the truth, that she loved him. But she couldn't—the words wouldn't come. The risk of humiliation was too great, because if he loved her, why wouldn't he tell her? There was nothing in his stance, in his expression, in his words to indicate anything other than a man calling off a business deal.

But she needed to at least try to give him a chance, a hint to tell her if he had any feelings for her at all. 'For you to manage with another woman?' she asked. 'Is it that easy for you?'

She'd swear he winced, rocked backwards on the balls of his feet, but then he steadied himself, shook his head. 'No. It's not easy. I swear it. But one day, yes, I will need to marry someone.' The words were delivered in an even pitch, and all of a sudden she recalled their conversation from weeks ago.

'I am upset in the same way I would be if a deal fell through. It's an...'

'Inconvenience? And you'll be looking for a new partner forthwith?'

'No! Not forthwith,' he answered her now. 'Of course I won't.'

'But in the fullness of time. A month? Three months?' Hearing the bitterness in her voice, she knew she had to pull back; she would never let him know how she felt, she had too much pride to open herself up to mortification again—so better to keep this pain to herself and treat her wounds in private. Her pain was not his fault, she knew that, and right now he was going through enough.

And so she pulled herself together. 'Rob, I

am sorry. I don't know what else to say.' Except that she loved him. 'But I am sure, I really am, that you will find a solution, that treatment will be successful, or maybe you will be plain lucky. With whoever you marry.'

Those words cost her more than she could say and she saw something fleeting across his blue eyes, a shadow of what was surely sorrow and pain.

'I didn't want it to work out this way. I am so sorry that I can't come through for you, that I can't fulfil my part of the bargain. More sorry than I can convey to you.'

She looked at him, saw and heard the sincerity in the catch in his voice, and she knew that any minute now she would either break down in tears or throw herself at his chest. Instead she stepped forward. 'Goodbye, Rob. Thank you for the past few weeks…thank you for…everything.' She slipped her engagement ring off her finger and handed it to him. 'And I hope it all works out for you.'

A gulp and she turned and walked away.

Three days later

Adriana clicked the link to join the video meeting and seconds later saw the familiar face of her sister. Stella looked tired, but even in her tiredness her beauty shone through. Her smile was tentative, her eyes worried as she surveyed Adriana.

'Ria, what happened?'

'Rob and I called it off.'

'Why? Because you couldn't go through with a marriage of convenience? That's OK.'

'It doesn't matter why. I really don't want to talk about it.' The last thing she wanted to do was discuss her own sorry state. She had done her best the last few days to throw herself into work on the estate by day, and by night she painted, sketched, but to her own horror all she could picture as she drew was Rob, had found herself trying to draw his forearm in charcoal, to capture the expression on his face...until she'd given up. 'I'd rather talk about you. Are you OK? Have you decided what to do?'

'No.' Stella gave a small laugh. 'I don't want to talk about me. All I still know is that I want this baby and as each day goes by I love her or him more.' She stopped. 'Oh, Ria, what did I say? I'm sorry.'

'It's fine.' Only it wasn't. She was happy for Stella—she really was. But suddenly she thought of how Rob must have felt when the specialist told him he may not be able to have children and her heart twisted.

'No, clearly it isn't fine. Are you worried you can't have a baby? Is that why you split up with Rob?'

'No!' But her sister's suggestion set off a train of thoughts in her head. If she had found out she had fertility issues, what would she have done? She would have called off the marriage exactly as Rob had. Would have assumed, no, would have known that it made the marriage a non-starter.

'Then what happened? Please talk to me. Because I feel all this is my fault. You don't need to feel bad that you called it off. You shouldn't have to go through a marriage of convenience, just to have a baby. You do not have to sacrifice yourself for Salvington. I told you that.'

The words pinged a lightbulb in her brain. 'I know, Stella. And I know you only want what's best for me. I am truly happy for you and I think you are going to be a wonderful mother, whether you do this on your own or somehow with the baby's father being involved. But listen, I've just realised something important. There's no time to explain right now but there is something I have to go and do.'

* * *

Rob eyed his parents in disbelief. 'You want me to do what?'

His father returned his glare with a basilisk one of his own. 'You heard us. Your mother has arranged a date for you with Lady Eleanor.'

'Let me ask another question. Why?'

His mother had the grace to at least look a little uncomfortable. 'I realise it seems a little soon, but your fertility issues mean we have to get a move on. It took your father and me so long and it was so hard and stressful I just want you to get started as soon as possible.'

'And Eleanor is happy to go along with this.'

'Well, obviously you would have to discuss it with her.' The Countess shrugged. 'Darling, you are the one who stood here a month ago and told us you wanted to get married as soon as possible to someone suitable, that you planned to "broker a deal" that would lead to a convenient marriage. That you would provide Darrow with an heir and you would take over the estate. When Stella dropped out you moved on to Adriana and...'

Rob closed his eyes. What an arrogant, misguided, pompous idiot he'd been. But that had been before Adriana, before she'd shown him so much. 'That was different. I didn't really

know Stella. I got to know Adriana and I can't
and won't just move on from her.'

There was a pause and his parents exchanged glances.

'That's what I came here to tell you. That
I'm shelving marriage plans. I will still take
over the estate—but I will also be pursuing
something else. When I was away for those
two years I set up a company—it's called Easel
Enterprises and I am truly proud of what I
achieved.' He hesitated and then ploughed forward. 'I hope if you are willing to listen to
more about it that you will be proud as well.'

He waited, watched them both.

Adriana met her mother's gaze. 'Are you sure
it's OK for me to see him?' she asked.

Her mother nodded. 'I think it's best. He
knows everything and he said he wants to see
you.'

'OK.' Trepidation touched her but she leaned
over to give her mother a kiss. 'I wanted to say
thank you as well, Mum.'

'Why?'

'For everything you've always done for me.
You've always loved me and I'm sorry Salvington has made your life difficult, and also
thank you for everything you said about my

marriage to Rob. I didn't understand at the time but I do now.'

Her mother returned her hug with fervour and then Adriana left her, walked up the stairs to her father's room, pushed open the door and entered.

'Father. How are you feeling?'

'Not so bad. Your mother is looking after me. Better than I deserve.' Her father surveyed her, an expression she couldn't read on her face. 'I wanted to talk to you. It was good of you to try to go through with the marriage to Rob. I wish it had worked.'

'So do I.' She waited for his expected outbreak of wrath, of jibes of anger at her failure, but none came.

Instead he sighed. 'It's OK. I'm too tired to be angry and I know I've no right to be anyway. The heart attack—it's changed me.'

'It's good you're not angry but I still think you should fight. Fight the law like you always have, use your influence. And...' She hesitated. 'I've got something for you.' Nerves clenched her tummy, even as she told herself what she knew to be true. That his opinion didn't matter. Just as Rob had told her. She handed over a framed painting, one of her favourites that she'd painted, a woodland picture of part of the Salvington estate.

Her father took it and looked down at it. 'This is very good. Who is the artist—' He broke off as he saw her name in the corner. 'Thank you,' was all he said, and she nodded.

'I'll be back soon,' she said and turned for the door.

Rob felt his phone vibrate in his pocket, nearly ignored the sensation. Realised he couldn't. It could be Fleur, finalising arrangements for the launch. A muted sense of excitement touched him, but somehow everything seemed muted without Adriana. He'd spent days walking around Darrow, taking solace from his land in a way he would never have believed possible. He'd thrown himself into the launch plans as well.

But always at the back of his mind was Adriana, her look of hurt when he'd spoken of marrying someone else. But what else could he have done? And what could he do now? Except miss her, and he did. He missed her with a constant ache, one he had no idea how to assuage.

He pulled his phone out of his pocket and

looked down at it, and his heart gave a sudden lurch. It was from Adriana. He scanned the message.

Hi Rob. It's urgent. Please could you come to Salvington at your earliest convenience? Adriana

Pausing only to reply, On my way, he dropped his phone back into his pocket, turned and headed at speed for the house. Once there he climbed straight into his car and headed for Salvington, pulling onto the sweep of driveway as soon as was humanly possible.

Braked as he saw Adriana standing a little distance from the house. Tried to calm the pounding of his heart, tried to hide the wave of bittersweet joy at seeing her as he drank in every detail of her—jeans, a white T-shirt, hair clipped back with the red barrettes he'd given her, a tentative smile on her face as he opened the car door and climbed out.

'Is everything OK?'

'Yes, it is. I think. I hope. Thank you for coming. I'm sorry to have summoned you like this. But I didn't really know what else to do. Anyway, is it OK if we walk whilst I try and explain?'

'Of course.' He couldn't help the smile that tipped his lips for a fleeting moment—it was so lovely to hear her voice.

'I wanted to show you some of Salvington,' she said as they began to walk, leaving the house behind them.

Was she perhaps showing him that she knew he'd been right to call off the marriage, show him what he had saved, thank him in some way? He didn't know and in truth right now he didn't care, was happy to be with her for one last time, happy that she was OK. Though of course there was a tiny bit of him that felt affronted that, whilst he had spent the past days hurting, she seemed to have recovered completely.

But then again, he loved her—she didn't love him.

As they walked she pointed out various spots to him, places she'd roamed as a child, places she'd sketched, places she'd seen different birds or wildlife. The places where she'd picked wild mushrooms and berries, the time she'd tried to fish for trout using a stick, a piece of string and a worm.

Until they came to a leafy glade.

'This was your favourite tree?' He hazarded a guess.

'Yup. And look.'

She led him further forward and he saw that under the wide stretch of branches she'd set a sylvan scene. The green leaves were dappled by the sunshine that made it through the canopy, but she'd also strung lights at differing heights to overhang a wooden picnic bench. The table had an array of covered dishes on it and in the centre was a wine cooler. The whole area was sprinkled with rose petals.

He halted, knew confusion was written on his features.

'Sit,' she said. 'Please.'

Once he was seated she sat too, opposite him so they could see each other clearly.

'I told you it was urgent,' she said. 'And it is. I just don't know where to start but I'll try.' She took a deep breath and then, 'I wanted to tell you this here, at Salvington. I wanted to show you the place I love. Because I do love Salvington and when I came to see you after Father's heart attack I did mean everything I said, about wanting to save it, about it being the most important thing to me.'

'I get that,' he said. 'I really do.'

'But now things have changed.'

He frowned, saw her hand instinctively go up to her barrettes as if to free her fringe, and then she didn't. Placed her hand on the table instead and kept her beautiful grey eyes on him, meeting his gaze full on.

'Because somewhere in the last few weeks I fell in love with you. And that changes everything.'

He could only stare at her as his brain tried to fathom the words, as happiness, joy started to seep through him, even as he tried to stem the tide. Adriana loved him. He needed to speak, to say something, but before he could she raised a hand.

'I need to finish, to say what I need to say. You see, when you told me what the specialist said I didn't even give Salvington a thought. I only cared about you and I cared about us. I wanted to be with you, I wanted to be by your side. I didn't want to lose you. And that was more important to me than Salvington and it still is. And I thought… I want you to know that.'

He knew he had to say something. 'Adriana, I love you.' Perhaps he should have dressed it up more, perhaps he shouldn't have blurted it out, but he couldn't bear for her not to know for even a second longer than necessary. 'I love you,' he repeated. 'I love you.'

He could see the joy dawn in her eyes, see a

hint of disbelief, and he reached out, said the words again. 'I love you. With all my heart. I've loved you since… I don't know when. But when the specialist told me the news about my fertility all I could think of was what it meant for us. That it meant I couldn't marry you, and then I knew that I loved you.'

'Why didn't you tell me?'

'Because I didn't want my love to be a burden to you. I didn't want your pity, or for you to feel you owed me anything, and I knew that for you Salvington would have to come first.' He hesitated. 'And how can you be so sure that isn't true? Your love, our love means too much to me to watch it go sour, to see your unhappiness…'

She shook her head. 'It won't. I can see things more clearly now. I was speaking to Stella and she thought I'd pulled out of our marriage because I didn't want a marriage of convenience. But this isn't a marriage of convenience to me—not any more.'

'Adriana, I…'

'My mother told me not to give up on the fairy tale for Salvington and she was right. To her, Salvington is bricks and mortar and soil. To me it will always be more than that. And that's why I know this sounds mad but I know that Salvington itself doesn't want my misery to go on in its name. We need to still fight—and I will…fight to have the laws changed. Because that is the right way forward to try and save it. And if we happen to have a son in time, or Stella happens to find a suitable husband and they have a son, then great! But if we are lucky enough to have a child or children then I will consider myself blessed whenever they are born. And if we have no children, or a daughter, or four daughters, that's good with me.' Her face was serious now. 'But for me the most important thing is to be with you.'

His eyes searched hers. 'You're sure? Because I'm optimistic that there is a good chance with time I can have a child, but there is no guarantee.'

'I know that.' Her expression was solemn. 'And I know that must be hard for you to come to terms with.'

'It is, but not for Darrow's sake. I already know that there is more to life than Darrow, more to it even than Easel. You made me imagine the joys of building tree houses, spending time with my children, letting them climb trees. They can enjoy the land, but then they can go and do whatever they want. And if I can't have children naturally then we could adopt. I know adopted children can't inherit titles, but hell, maybe we can lobby to change that law too. And if we can't our children would still be happy.'

'I completely agree. And I think adoption is an amazing idea. But the most important thing is that we are together and we can make all those decisions together. If you'll have me.'

He wondered if it were possible for his heart to burst with joy, because he heard nothing but truth in her words, knew there had been nothing but truth in his.

Moving round the table, he got down on one knee and pulled her engagement ring out of his pocket, where he'd kept it for the past few days.

'Will you marry me and make me the happiest man in the world?'

'I will.' Her answer was clear, uttered without even a hint of doubt.

'And I promise to love and cherish you for the rest of my life.' He slipped the ring on her finger and then sat down beside her, one arm wrapped around her. 'You've changed me, Adriana. Shown me how to trust, shown me how to find a connection with Darrow, shown me what having a family truly means. You've brought joy to my life.'

'And you've shown me that it is possible to

embrace a life outside of Salvington, to have belief in myself. To believe in my art. If I want to go to college, if I want to study, I can. You've shown me that I am a worthy person in my own right, that I am my sister's equal, that I can be a countess.'

'You will be the most loved Countess in the land,' he said, and as he kissed her, and then as they ate and drank and discussed their future, planned a fairy-tale happy-ever-after full of love, he knew that he was the luckiest man alive.

* * * * *

If you enjoyed this story, check out these other great reads from Nina Milne

Second Chance in Sri Lanka
The Secret Casseveti Baby
Whisked Away by the Italian Tycoon
Italian Escape with the CEO

All available now!